THE JINGLE BELL PRINCIPLE

The Jingle Bell Principle

MIROSLAV HOLUB

TRANSLATED BY
James Naughton

BLOODAXE BOOKS

ISBN: 1 85224 123 3

First published 1992 by
Bloodaxe Books Ltd,
P.O. Box 1SN,
Newcastle upon Tyne NE99 1SN.

First published in Czech in 1987 by Melantrich, Prague.

Bloodaxe Books Ltd acknowledges
the financial assistance of Northern Arts.

Cover reproduction by V & H Reprographics, Newcastle upon Tyne.

Cover printing by J. Thomson Colour Printers Ltd, Glasgow.

Printed in Great Britain by
Bell & Bain Limited, Glasgow, Scotland.

Contents

Pereant qui ante nos nostra dixerunt.
To the devil with those that published before us.
AELIUS DONATUS
4th century

The Rules of Writing Short Columns

After a few years writing short columns I discovered that what I was writing were short columns; up till then I had imagined I was simply writing in such a way as to stop after 43 lines, because there wasn't room for any more. The fact that I was fitting a literary genre into its set dimensions charmed, flattered and disconcerted me. I began to look into the rules and fundamentals of the genre. Finding however no satisfactory profound teaching on this genre, I did some thinking myself about the ways of these columns, as I infer them from the products of some more expert pens.

Of the rules I have found I offer you these:

1. Above all let the column be of a light disposition. It is inappropriate to use 43 lines to expatiate on gloomily emotional states, for gloomy emotions have a habit of overflowing their banks immeasurably. A light disposition still permits one to deal with the dark side of things too, within decent limits, a tip here, a tap there, and quickly on with the show.

2. As far as possible, give the column a certain facetiousness. A facetious tone obviates the necessity of any broader logical analysis, unfit for the format, and releases one from deeper probing of what is called inward reality, entailing multi-volumed recherches du temps perdu.

3. Let the topic be fairly mundane and minimal in matter. To treat of the sinking of the *Titanic* within the confines of a short column is a literary faux pas. To treat of a small boat, aging motorcar with a low number of cylinders, or bathing in a lesser sea is much more stylish and rewarding from the literary standpoint, for this has been done for generations.

4. If we must choose what are termed more demanding topics, such as science, problems of the communal order of primitive society, or the pollution of the atmosphere, one must draw explicitly on personal experience, which gives the material a down-to-earth quality and imbues it with the warmth of humorous narrative. By consistent personalising of the subject matter we thus ensure that no one takes any of it personally. In this respect a short column

piece is more of a brief visit to the zoo than an expedition to the jungle.

5. It follows from this, that as a genre the short column is pink-cheeked, hale and hearty, recreational and thoroughly recommendable for hygienic purposes. The writing and consumption of short columns in a state of acute stomach upset is a contradiction in terms. Let the short column be the fruit of physiological satiety and verisimilitude. Hunger for paradox is more conducive to poetry, neurotic want of appetite to the novel. Collected papers presuppose a bilious diet.

These then are some of the rules of writing short columns. It bothers me a lot that I haven't followed them more closely.

The Function of the Motorcycle

A motorcycle functions entirely in accordance with the laws of reason, and a study of the art of motorcycle maintenance is really a miniature study of the art of rationality itself.
ROBERT PIRSIG
1974

QUÉBEC 76
M-87384

> **The habit of apprehending a technology in its completeness: this is the essence of technological humanism, and this is what we should expect education in higher technology to achieve...the path to culture should be through a man's specialism, not by-passing it.**
>
> LORD ERIC ASHBY
> 1958

In Defence of the Motor-Car

The motor-car: 1. is the goal, nay the acme of petit-bourgeois strivings after conspicuous appurtenances; 2. replaces the desirable mobility of the body (and spirit) by the sedentary mode of life; 3. disturbs the tranquillity of nature and inundates the urban scene with its poisonous exhalations; 4. collides with other motor cars and objects in general.

However: 1. Petit-bourgeois behaviour was not brought about by the motor-car, it merely becomes the victim of it, and that will pass. 2. Spinal deformities and haemorrhoids also existed beforehand, and someone who fails to grasp the basic need for physical exercise and sport will hardly be persuaded of this by an empty garage. 3. Undisturbed tranquillity of nature can only be consumed on the supposition that we can get there somehow; we also have to get to town somehow or other too, and nobody would be as eccentric as to crawl along in an overheated motor-car through clouds of noxious gases if he could get there better some other way, and that may also one day come to pass. 4. The car is not self-propelled in the sense of getting up to its own little escapades, these are perpetrated by its most sensitive component, generally termed the motorist or car-driver.

In the very principle of car-driving I see in fact the definite positive value of the motor-car in the progressive humanisation of the ape. For driving basically provides the closest – one might almost say natural contact between people and machines on a mass scale. People learn to understand the language of machines and in so doing develop power and personal responsibility. Material momentum and velocity even. They learn to react and make decisions, and I don't know if it can be shown statistically, but I would lay bets that a good driver, especially one who has been driving since the minimum legal age, acquires reduced reaction time, enhanced psychomotor tempo, adaptability, sometimes even self-criticism and self-control. Components in other words of trained intelligence and moral volition. Last but not least, in constant contact with the rules of the highway code he learns, or is obliged to learn, exactitude in their fulfilment and in their application to ever new and unexpected situations. For every ten kilometres he must encounter such glaring examples of bad driving, indiscipline and idiotic behaviour that one would think it a hardened soul indeed that could fail to learn the lesson that law observance, adequate technique and fair play are the sine qua non of the survival of matter on the highways of life.

Men and times of evil,
Nothing more is right.
Little birds sit on your shoulders
And sing me through the night.
KENNETH PATCHEN
1960

Pathways

Mice make pathways in the grass and tunnels in turf. They run about in them immutably, identically, there and back, day (night) after day (night). They are silly creatures, with limited mental horizons. Driven off their path by an artificial barrier they become confused and strive in every way possible to get back on to the good old familiar route. Even the higher mammals do likewise, they beat their pathways, yes mark them too and follow the scent as they run always the same way, there and back. Obstacles upset them, they are disturbed in their behaviour and tenor of life.

Strangely enough people, both country people and town people, do likewise, however superior they may be in status to the mice, and even though beating a path and scent-marking hardly come into it. I'm sure we all know or can easily see that we always follow any habitually repeated route subconsciously in the same manner. Here and only here do we cross the street, here we take the short-cut across what was once grass, here we turn a corner. Without special reason or motivation we fail to alter our pathways. Some even measure their steps and place their feet always on the same paving stones, right foot on the dark slabs, left on the light, and with some – presumably somewhat weaker – individuals the thing becomes a ritual, whose breaking signals inclement fate just like a spider seen first thing in the morning or a black cat which runs across the road.

A psychological experiment of this nature was recently carried out in Prague, in Jungmann Square. The building of the metro caused the way through from Wenceslas Square to Jungmann Street to be blocked, and partly to the Street of 28th October also. Jungmann Square as such disappeared in barriers, piping, excavations and gentle mire. Coming from Wenceslas Square it was possible to go two different ways, but each led into the Church of Our Lady of the Snow and no further. This fact was unusually clearly and graphically displayed on large signs strategically placed. The vast majority of pedestrians habitually using this route simply read the signs – and ignored them. It was simply impossible to credit that the path might be blocked by an artificial barrier. The vast majority of pedestrians were shaken by this notice, but carried on just the same as before. The vast majority of pedestrians ended up in the Church of Our Lady of the Snow, some for the first time in their lives, and here they scouted around vainly for a way past the altar on to Jungmann Square.

I found myself in one such huddle of people taking this pathway. When we issued frustrated from the church, we met another huddle, evidently endowed with greater powers of criticism and rationality, for though they had also followed the old accustomed route now stopped up they asked us whether it led anywhere. Yes, we said resoundingly, straight to the sacristy. To our delighted joy these good people were unable to trust the full content of our words and accepted only our initial Yes...Shaken, they nevertheless continued on their way into the church.

Such is the force of established pathways. Both the written and the spoken word lose their signalling impact, juxtaposed to the instinct to continue on one's previous path. Only a physical barrier, here the wall of the church, compels us to react and casts us into the turmoil of mental activity required for the beating of a new, alternative pathway.

When the way through to Jungmann Square is again clear, our first foray in this direction will be hesitant and shy, our foot will step questioningly on the new paving, tasting, testing and doubting the stones, not believing our eyes, until the new path is well beaten and accustomed.

And some will perseverate and go on taking the detour which they beat in their minds during the period of impassability.

Great is the force of inertia of the path-beaten mind. And we have no other.

Experience is the name everyone gives to their mistakes.
OSCAR WILDE
1854-1900

The Frail Regularity of the World

The everyday order of the world differs from the large-scale order of the world in that we experience the former at every step, whereas we perceive the latter only as an object of study. Whereas we accept and register changes in the latter without difficulty, for the everyday world we demand a certain accustomed order and regularity, without which existence becomes somehow impossible.

I have never met anyone who felt somehow deeply affected by the fact that the law of parity does not apply for weak interactions. In the same way the discovery of somatic mutations and laboratory production of allophenic mice bother nobody. As far as the cosmos goes, there are even those who still consider carrier rockets and the lunar surface to be mere trick cinematography.

On the other hand even very slight variations in the simple course of everyday life leave deep marks in us: on the southern edge of Prague, for example, there is a very busy main road equipped on its right-hand side with a signpost indicating obligatory direction, pointing straight out into the fields, where you aren't supposed to go of course, because new housing estates are being built over there as far as the eye can see. No one obeys this sign of course, but I have seen many drivers whose vehicles and senses had come to a dead halt at this very spot, staring out with fixed gaze like Lot's wife. For a signpost of such a kind shatters the motorist's faith in the regularity of the world.

I can say in my own case, that I was deeply affected by the fact that the recipient of a posted item from me in the district Prague 6 had to pay additional postage due, as the stamps used, bought a week earlier in Prague 4, were declared invalid by the lady who delivered it. Here I felt collapse one of the unacknowledged buttresses supporting my everyday world. For if my stamps are no longer valid, it may well happen that some delivery person will declare my birth certificate invalid, and I shall have to declare myself nullified by official affidavit. Regarding the issue of stamps, I enquired of the ministry responsible and received an assurance that all stamps issued since 1953 remain valid for postal purposes. The regularity of my everyday life was thereby restored, but that terrible insight into how little is needed for its erosion lives with me still.

Besides, the revision of the principle of parity was only feasible on the presupposition that postage stamps and traffic signposts kept their validity. In this way the order of the micro-world meets the large-scale order of the macro-world most intimately.

> **For there was never yet philosopher**
> **That could endure the toothache patiently.**
> WILLIAM SHAKESPEARE
> 1564-1616

Flies

On his journey across the planet and through history man has encountered above all the fly. Of all the animal realm the fly is mankind's most faithful follower, alighting doubtless with the same fervour on Lucy (Australopithecus afarensis) as on Laura and Juliet, on Peking Man as on Confucius, on our Přemysl the Ploughman as on our Matthew Beetle, distinguishing not between Agamemnon and the Achaeans who fell at his bidding before the mighty walls of Troy, and it would certainly have settled upon Homer, assuming he existed, and disturbed him with all its fly-like diligence from his regular hexameters. For the historic mission of flies is, apart from the transmission of a smallish number of infectious agents, the disturbance of hexameter producers, of cultural values in general: I should like to know where we would be in terms of cultural riches today, if its creators had not had to fidget, invent fly swats and fly paper, if they had been able to concentrate to the full, undistracted by waving of arms, invention of curses and fascinated tracking of this two-winged buzzer, which evidently considers its prime goal in life to be settling on a human leg here and there laid bare, on a labouring hand or a meditating bald pate.

It is no wonder that the fly has inveigled itself into a large number of our proverbs. If there are a lot of us about somewhere, we are like flies (not marmots, or aphids, and certainly not streptococci, ever-present as they may be upon the human surface), if we are debilitated, we are weak as a fly (despite its impressive energy), if we are at the mercy, we are 'flies come and take me' (not bears, or the itch mite, undoubtedly more adept at devouring), if we are capricious, we are giddy as a fly, and if we bring off a double feat, we kill two flies with a single blow. If we have anything other than ourselves on our mind and on our tongue, then it is the fly, that harmless and good-hearted vampire of philosophers' thoughts, that real disturber of Sleeping Beauty's slumbers, that public looter of lovers' sought-after seclusion, that defenceless nothing that settles on Hercules' armpit at the very moment he raises his cudgel to slay the Lernaean Hydra. When I try to put myself into the tricky predicament of Prometheus, I sense that his great punishment was not so much the eagle gouging out the liver from his body chained to the rock, as the fly tenderly busy at the drop of sweat on the genius's perspiring brow.

There is nothing at all about this of course in the legend, but that is the precise crux of the matter: the fly is an example of an historic factor so absurd it can only be granted proverbial, never mythopoeic status. Myths are for eagles; flies in the ointment cannot be admitted.

Nevertheless: how many eagles do we have? And how many flies?

> **Year by year we are becoming better equipped to accomplish the things we are striving for. But what are we actually striving for?**
> BERTRAND DE JOUVENEL
> 1970

On Inseparable Baggage

The idea of a human person as a figure from head to foot and from the end of the fingers of the left hand to the end of the fingers of the right, a figure bounded by a casing of skin and clothes, is quite unreal. Wherever I look, I find no such figures. The human person in reality comprises both figure and accompanying baggage. Sometimes several items of baggage, but these as far as may be are generally off-loaded in the cloakroom, leaving only the indivisible or inseparable baggage on the person. With this, the elongation or extension of the person, the individual ends, or even begins. Inseparable baggage in this land of ours constitutes a briefcase, bag or satchel, in cases of enhanced elegance some kind of bijou baguette containing cash, identity requirements and clutter. The briefcases and satchels contain the same, only the clutter is quantitatively and qualitatively more advanced.

Indivisible baggage is only cast off in exceptional circumstances and during special occasions and ceremonies at which we consequently feel awkward and uncomfortable. Which only goes to show that indivisible baggage is the basis and guarantor of our uniqueness.

For the clutter contained in indivisible luggage is something so personal and non-transferable, that in this respect only the papillary lines on fingers and the main transplantation antigens on cell membranes can compete.

Ladies' clutter consists above all of a certain amount of make-up and smelling stuff, possibly coins mixed in with combs, nail-clippers and tweezers, also scraps of paper with telephone numbers of unknown origin, unused notepads and cuttings with recipes for Serbian filet French-style and French skin milk Serbian-style.

Gentlemen's clutter is comprised above all of unsettled documents including letters, bunches of keys to the gates of heaven and hell, amongst which useful and used keys vanish into the unknown, a rusty penknife, half-read pamphlets, a largish number of wallets with indefinite contents of expired validity, amongst the better-provided a folding umbrella, congealed cough lozenges and a spare bag in case of bulky acquisition of more basic clutter. There are of course well-known cases of a gentleman being in a permanent state of dual briefcasedness, this constituting the extension of a peculiarly labyrinthine personality.

Even children frequently by instinctive imitation embark on a diminutive extension to their persona, and this then contains especially pebbles set in shapeless chocolate and the legs of long-serving puppets.

The kind of indivisible luggage chosen is less governed by the person than its contents. There are some who alternate between a diplomatic attaché case and a shoppers' tote-bag, of course in view of the awkward transferability of inside clutter preference is normally given to one piece of luggage over a longer period of time, sometimes stretching to eternity.

And as we depart thither, let us observe how tremendously poignant and utterly dead are these inseparable – and parted-from impedimenta, which remain as a metaphysical extension, when the body itself falls into anonymous nakedness and final diagnosis. For the body (and the spirit) is merely a by-product and interconnection of the uniqueness of genes, molecules and inseparable baggage.

Progress was all right; it only went on too long.

JAMES THURBER

1894-1961

The Instructive Camera-Case

One of the great problems of objects in general is that they have certain properties which, though inessential, are at the same time insuperable. For example, an essential feature of an aquarium is that it holds and transparently keeps fish, but an inessential and insuperable property is that it cracks under the influence of ultrasonic waves, which leads to such disruption of its essential property that on occasion we find our goldfish browsing in the encyclopaedia which stood below the aquarium and whose essential property is to contain encyclopaedic articles, and inessential, but in the given conditions insuperable one, to contain goldfish. Whereas the water is found by the owner of the flat beneath you, and he is found as a rule entirely immune to any theoretical treatise on the inessential properties of aquaria and the futility of fighting them.

A textbook example of an inessential and insuperable property is the leather Roleiflex camera-case which has engraved itself in the annals of our family. After acquiring this reflex camera our family deemed it unworthy to be housed in just any old case; the outer casing being in the Czech context the most important part of any object. So a tremendously pukka casing of calf or whatever was duly ordered. I don't remember exactly what. But what I do remember most clearly is that when this luxurious photographic receptacle was delivered, around it there spread the most unimaginable stink. A stink so powerful, that it was more of a shriek. A shriek of a stink as calf-like as it was yeasty, not to say putrefying.

After expert consultation an attempt was made at decontamination. This consisted of filling the bag with chlorinated lime, enveloping it in chlorinated lime and enclosing it in a box with chlorinated lime. After a month's immersion in this bleach the case was taken out and scrubbed. At this point it was found that the original stink remained and announced its presence unabated, but had acquired a further new quality, that of chlorinated lime.

After prolonged airing in the garden (a practice somewhat at odds with the principles of nature conservation), when it was found that in a stronger north-westerly breeze the lime at least was less noticeable, we proceeded – after further expert advice of course – to carry out onion decontamination. Approximately one kilogram of sliced onion was brought into long-term contact with the casing. The result was that the bag stank still of its previous bleachy odour, likewise however of onion, in the manner of tear-gas, so that even the eye of the camera misted over in consequence.

The insuperable receptacle was thereupon placed alone and empty in a cellar with a notable draught. Because this was war-time, we soon fell into suspicion of hoarding excessive and illegal supplies of meat and onions.

After the war my father tried just once to use the bag. It shows clearly in the photographs. Grandma, who never really held with photography anyway, henceforth refused to have her picture taken ever again. She claimed it was bad for her eyesight.

And so the camera bag was laid aside permanently. I believe my father secretly buried it.

It was therefore not only an insuperable bag, but also an instructive one: there exist qualities, however inessential, which simply cannot be masked over. The masking of insuperable inessential properties simply leads to the creation of further inessential properties, and in the end you just have to bury the whole lot in the ground.

> **Clever people bring into this world**
> **the heroic idea of unlimited possibilities;**
> **clots however bring and uphold the epic,**
> **even fairy-tale notion**
> **of unlimited difficulties, accidents, obstacles and oppositions.**
> KAREL ČAPEK
> 1925

On the Topology of Bits and Bobs

Strange are the paths of development of the human spirit. I know a good number of people who have mastered the laws of thermodynamics and set theory. I also have friends familiar with molecular genetics. Some are experts in legal matters, many in the theory of art. My neighbour K.E. is knowledgeable about historic churches, my neighbour A.B. is a master of poultry keeping. But none of these, neither the people of theory, nor the people of practice, ever have any precise idea as to where they put their cash receipt, or as to whether the hammer is with the pliers or wherever he last left the box of nails.

My neighbour M.M., who is such a skilled chess player that he remembers the moves of whole matches and enjoys talking about Euwe's application of Nimcovič's Indian Defence, the other day lost the key to the room where he keeps his chess set. Since playing matches in his head was somewhat irksome even to him, he set about searching his memory and came up with the theory that the said key had been placed in the pocket of the coat he had taken out into the garden to dust. This action, as theoretically reconstructed, had two possible consequences. Firstly, he might have carried the coat the wrong way up, so that the key fell out even as he walked, secondly, he might have carried the coat in the normal position, that is to say collar up, but during dusting the key might have been expelled. In either case the key was presumably located somewhere outside, where a certain amount of snow had just fallen. So that the key lost while walking or expelled during dusting was buried, along with the traces of walking and dusting. Neighbour M.M. carried out several probes in the approximate likely vicinity, but without success. M.M. therefore came to the practically important and theoretically reasoned conclusion, that the room with the chess set would be inaccessible until the snow thawed, for his other key was mislaid with other further keys in a place unknown.

With the calm characteristic of fine chess players M.M. awaited the onset of spring, devoting himself to the solving of two-movers in his head. Spring's arrival gave ample proof of the perspicacity of his thinking. The key was discovered in burgeoning weeds only two metres away from the place of probable dusting. After cleansing with the help of rust remover the key was usable again and the room unlocked. After expulsion of spiders and other Arthropods neighbour M.M. was able calmly to continue his match of Hort versus Spassky.

I use this instance of the interaction between neighbour M.M. and the key to his room as evidence for the belief which has been growing within me in recent times, that the human mind is more and more well adapted to dealing with the relativistic principles of the structure of the universe and the applications of pre-stressed concrete, but still just as helpless in the disposition of its own bits and bobs. Leaving you to this little thought of mine, I now go to search for the lid to my typewriter. In theory it should be next to the collected works of Charles Dickens.

I need no assurances...
I do not doubt that temporary affairs keep on and on millions of years.
I do not doubt that interiors have their interiors and exteriors have their exteriors...

WALT WHITMAN
1819-1892

The Holy Rite of Waiting

Even if we count only actual true waiting in waiting-rooms, in front of waiting-rooms, in front of cash desks, in front of windows, under windows, or simply outside doors, it may be estimated that we spend in this fashion at least a full 200 long days in the course of one single ordinary life. Compared with other non-working and incidental activities this is assuredly no paltry length of time, and one might expect that up-and-coming generations would be trained purposely for such a significant proportion of their lives and such a frequently practised activity, just as people are trained in fire prevention, although with the best will in the world fires still take up less of our time. Of course extinguishing fires involves saving life and property, whereas waiting apparently does not. Unless one is prepared to admit that waiting is actually burning up one's time of life.

The generations however are not trained for waiting, they do not undergo appropriate exercises and examinations, and each individual enters waiting- rooms totally unprepared, untrained, uneducated and forced to resort to improvisation and personal experience.

Wait-training ought primarily to consist of basic instruction about waiting premises. These are as a rule dingy, ill-adapted, furnished with a very limited number of places, not to say seats, with cast-off adornments from elsewhere and intellectual nourishment in the context of which a month-old newspaper in some more venerable Arabic dialect constitutes true entertainment. For reasons of economy waiting premises are normally kept in semi-darkness, effectively restricting any reading or other work brought from home. For one of the fundamental features of waiting is, that it is an act-

ivity focussed on its desired goal, that is on penetrating through to the official, medical or other specific act required, and it must be an activity to some extent self-torturing, masochistic, something like purgatory and ecstatic sublimation of ordinary activities, thoughts, anxieties and joys.

The only activity actually to be carried on is the monitoring of those who were there already, with a view to guessing whether they are waiting on the same basis as you or not, or merely assisting someone else in waiting, this coupled especially with the monitoring of those who arrived after you, to prevent them jumping the queue, for jumping the queue is the great dream and comforting metaphysical hope of every person in waiting. For this reason waiting is a very oddly and narrowly specialised activity, demanding the whole person's attention. It is inadmissible to wait in a half-hearted fashion. Those who leave themselves an escape route, by being ready to leave if things start taking too long, are artful dodgers, who do not deserve to be served; they should be marked down and excluded from all further waiting.

In properly executed waiting all oscillations of the conscious mind are eliminated and brought down to a single level, the attention fixes on a single spot, such as the doorhandle, and vegetative functions and reactions are suppressed. Wise guys who fancy spending part of this sacred time on the W.C. rightly and properly lose their place in the line.

Wait-training ought therefore to include certain principles of yoga, learning off by heart passages from handbooks of Zen Buddhism, mental exercises in descents into nothingness and physical exercises in total self-denial and self-oblivion while maintaining one's place in the queue and all the appearance of an individual fit for reception or admission.

And here I have a suggestion, a proposition tested by hundreds of entire long days of waiting, which commits no sacrilege to the ceremonial and ritual of waiting and leaves its necessary equilibrium undisturbed: In every concrete waiting-room, and in every concrete given form of waiting, think up some concrete way in which this waiting period, without disrespect to the genius loci et temporis, might be shortened or completely eliminated.

I warn of course against communicating the said invented means to the relevant party. Here you would immediately find out several dozen reasons why this is impossible in the given instance, and you would cause essential harm to the impending long-awaited transaction. Just think about this method quietly to yourself. And try it out maybe, when others are waiting for you.

I shall subtract it from the past...
TADEUSZ RÓŻEWICZ
1953

A Land Pleasant in Clime to Inhabit

It rained. 40 mm of rain fell upon us. It got in our shoes. The cellars filled with water up to the steps. The fruits of the fields lay in puddles, nay in marshes, to the detriment of their health. Transport was overcrowded, some forms even leaked water in, so that they collapsed. It ran down the chimneys. The stucco suffered, to the detriment of buildings' health also.

After that it failed to rain for ten days. The wind raised up clouds of dust. The respiratory tracts suffered. The fruits of the field hung their heads, and suffered to the detriment of their health. Transport overheated and collapsed in quantity. Stucco dried and peeled. Tar on the roof melted and dripped down the facade. Cracks developed between panels. Water levels dropped in wells. Housing estates, inhabitants and livestock included, suffered to the detriment of their health. Sunstrokes were a daily occurrence.

Winter came. It was chill, without snapping, nevertheless the pipes froze, winter crops were harmed, and ice cracked walls forming picturesque crazy patterns. Cold infections filled the waiting-rooms, there were power failures, and heating failures. Transport failed to start.

After that some snow fell. Forest giants, bending under the unexpected weight, broke. The fruits of the field showed every sign of mouldering, roads became impassable or over-salted, so that transport either did not run, or rusted. Roofs sagged and walls grew damp patches round the gutters. We got our shoes wet. Holiday-makers disregarding bans on hiking got lost in the mist.

According to the Bohemian chronicler Cosmas the tribal leader Czech once 'cast his sharp gaze over the hills and vales, slopes and plains', bade his followers set down the household gods they had brought with them on their shoulders, and told them to sacrifice a pleasing burnt-offering, for...'this is that land...as you observe yourselves, pleasant in clime to inhabit...'

There are just three possibilities: either the somewhat unperceptive leader Czech arrived with his people at a rare moment when it was neither pouring, nor was there drought, nor was it snowing, nor were chill frosts ruling the land, and quickly 'founded the first settlements' before the climate had managed to show its true colours. Or the said people and its functionaries and gods were somehow better adapted to the local climate in these true colours and employed more appropriate technologies. Or it was even worse elsewhere without so much as a place to set down the household gods.

In any event it is curious how over the last thousand years and a bit we have adapted so little to the given climate, both physically and technologically; how few of our weathers and indeed few of all possible weathers on all possible continents are in fact just right. Or with what age-old fixed obduracy we choose to believe that getting our shoes wet is not the natural state of mankind.

Wrinkles

Let us take care that age does not make more wrinkles
on our spirit than on our face.
MICHEL DE MONTAIGNE
1533-92

Hence to fight and conquer in all your battles is not supreme excellence; supreme excellence consists in breaking the enemy's resistance without fighting.

SUN TZE
5th-6th century BC

On Aggression

Konrad Lorenz wrote a whole book on the subject, but it only deals with animals. We have no such intention, but merely wish to observe that from time to time we are subject to certain strange visions:

Someone gets on a tram and (having punched his ticket) immediately fetches the driver one (What's all the delay?), the latter returns the compliment (What're you doing on my tram?), the new arrival hies over to a seat, kicks the person sitting thereon (What sort of a dumb fool hat is that?), then proceeds to trample underfoot the book of the young man sitting behind (What's all this provocative reading, I hate books!).

Or someone drives up to a petrol pump. Quickly he gets out, deftly rips off the wing mirror of the car in front (Why did you pass me like that, you clown?), kicks in the door of the car behind (Why did you creep up on me, you oaf?), whereupon those affected get out and puncture each other's tyres with prepared spikes, then everyone else's, and finally all proceed to demolish the modest petrol station kiosk, for they have run out of distilled water.

Or else the one in the supermarket who is last in the convoluted checkout queue raises a neigh like a horse, nimbly gets down on all fours and bites the calves of the waiting customers, who likewise engage each other in the manner of knightly joustings with laden trolleys, calling each other the sort of names Carl von Linnaeus could have used when devising his binary system of nomenclature. The cashier briskly adds surcharges to the cost of every item for the stock bones he is hurling about with such gay abandon.

These are of course only visions.

Visions however proceed from signs. If you look about you in situations such as I have indicated, the signs will scarcely elude your attention. Deeply hidden is the rapacity of the age, H. von Boderer once wrote. Just below the surface, one might add, just below the surface. I used to think that one of the sources of Central European aggressivity was a certain fondness for order and mass neurosis caused by the observance of regulations. But it is something else.

Something suppressed. The aggressive instincts are even triggered off by mere distaste for the appearance, accoutrements or attitude of others. They are even touched off by the mere existence of others, despite their being a sine qua non of our own existence.

In our own minds we tend to think that our aggressive feelings are caused mainly by the blockheadedness of others. This may well be so, but the process is circular, and all in all it may be stated that aggressivity is simply tantamount to blockheadedness. We think we are defending something. Unfortunately however that something is our own blockheadedness. Let us try to view our sharp-elbowed fellow citizens in this light. As well as ourselves.

It is quite unnecessary for me to bend and bow my reason, for that my knees will suffice.
MICHEL DE MONTAIGNE
1533-92

On Natural Respect

Youth should pay homage (as Karel Poláček puts it) to persons older, more distinguished or higher in rank. Older persons must pay homage to persons still older, the distinguished to those still more distinguished, the higher-ranking to those yet more high-ranking. A chain which is virtually without end. And yet it is the very basis of acceptable social behaviour.

Technically speaking, homage is to be given in an appropriate, commensurate manner. That is to say, neither in a servile nor in a superior way, neither casually nor ostentatiously. But here comes the question: commensurate to what? Commensurate to age, distinction and rank? How is this to be measured? I would say therefore, that commensurateness relates not to quantity of years or rungs in the social ladder, but to the respect that the person to whom homage is to be paid arouses in those who are to pay the homage. The basis lies in natural respect. Natural respect is evoked by a) the person's essential human character, b) the person's current social standing, that is to say, wisdom and good sense, heroic deeds, acts of self-sacrifice, responsible and responsibly occupied position in life.

As regards a) it must of course be noted that both aged men and babes in arms awaken the same basic respect. I may therefore state with an easy mind that I happily greet a schoolboy, and that I have not yet lived to see the day when I might expect to be greeted by anyone. In any case a properly behaved babe in arms evokes much greater respect in me than a tipsy old man. Equally, more respect is aroused by one who expects no greeting than one who does.

As regards b) it must be stressed that wisdom and self-sacrifice – as a basis of obligatory respect – are not revealed once and for all, but must constantly be demonstrated. The sources of respect are not something like the Order of the Garter, but an actual state of being.

If then older and more distinguished persons complain of the disrespect and hardened indifference of youth, they are complaining to a certain extent also of their own inability to evoke this respect. I fear that there is a decline in decency among us. I fear that it is not merely lack of upbringing, but also a lack of objects of respect, a lack of persons worthy of respect in the micro-environment of our lives. A lack of those who know that youth is no argument, and age even less.

It isn't that they can't see the solution.
It is that they can't see the problem.
G.K. CHESTERTON
1874-1936

Logical Riddles

Certain ancient riddles and puzzles documenting the limits of logic or the limits of certain minds have found their way straight into the history books. The story is well-known for example of the Cretan X.X. who comes along and says: 'All Cretans are liars.' So what is the truth, are they or aren't they? There is a solution however to another riddle, one which we set ourselves (evidently feeling playful and simple-minded) in our student days. A traveller comes to an island inhabited by two tribes. The members of one tribe always lie, while the members of the other always tell the truth. The traveller reaches a crossroads and wants to know which of two roads leads to the village of X. Stopping a native at the crossroads, but not knowing which of the tribes he belongs to, he asks him one single question and on the basis of the answer learns unambiguously and unerringly which is the correct road to take. What is his question? There are even two possible questions which work, maybe you know what they are.

Clearly in a mood of inadmissible playfulness and simple-mindedness, I began setting this second riddle to some of my acquaintances. I divided them provisionally into three groups. A) Simple-minded, and above all impractical people. B) People of ample intellect, skilled at decision-making, practical decision-making included. C) People of outstanding, nay omniscient wisdom, who never say do-not-know. I then divided these three groups into subgroups, to wit: 1. jokers, and 2. non-jokers.

The results are worth noting. Basically only jokers were willing to try to solve the puzzle. Non-jokers in groups A and B more or less politely declined, people in group B excusing themselves on grounds of lack of time and needing to repair their car distributor. Non-jokers in group C generally told me in no uncertain terms where to go, Crete for example. There were roughly the same proportions of successful jokers in both groups A and B. Group A jokers however spared neither time nor effort, whereas group B jokers felt irked, and when they failed to succeed right away, had a tendency to become temporary non-joker members of group C. One group A colleague has been working on the puzzle for over a month now, and from time to time he keeps me informed by telephone, when the latter is working. The smallest number of successful solvers was in group C.

From the results obtained I conclude that outstanding wisdom and omniscience are incompatible with the solving of new riddles, evidently because for people like that no new riddles exist, and what seems to us simple folk to be a riddle, is seen by them as simply nothing. I conclude likewise, that any group C people landing on the said island would have more than a thing or two to say to the natives about their preposterous ways.

Illiterates have to dictate.
STANISŁAW JERZY LEC
1964

Overweening Crassness

A young, affluently pudgy man at the wheel of a 1600cc vehicle, painted royal blue and plastered with stickers of a highly international calibre, drove up to the hospital gate. Because for understandable reasons private cars are forbidden entry to the hospital grounds, the motorist encountered a porter who came dashing up. The drift of the young man's arguments was that first he was coming to fetch an unusually sick patient and highly placed relative, second he had friends in the management, ministry and elsewhere. The porter was soon vanquished and opened the barrier pole. The affluently pudgy man drove round the whole site with great satisfaction neatly scattering ambulant patients and came to rest before the administrative wing, for here indeed he had an assignation with a young lady presently otherwise engaged within and otherwise in excellent good health.

He came to rest, slumped behind the wheel, lit up a ciggy and waited. The healthy young lady was of course still otherwise engaged and not yet on her way. Because the time of affluently pudgy young men who know their way around is precious, the present specimen decided to put a stop to this state of other engagement. Because getting out of the car and going to ask or arrange things is beyond the repertoire and station of men who know their way

around, he set about blowing his horn. The horn was naturally well endowed, stentorian and magisterial in tone and penetration. First he gave a long and a short blast, next three long ones and two short ones, and then one long continuous blast and another five short ones.

Recumbent patients, insofar as they were in a fit state, made their way to the windows and listened to the delightful music. A passing doctor expressed some reservations, but the trumpeting youngster told him uncompromisingly where to go. And the youngster hooted on, until the lady arrived. Then he started up and drove off, nodding lightly to the porter.

That's all.

Perhaps it's not worth mentioning, but I use this little set-piece in order to illustrate that type of behaviour, character or attitude which we shall term overweening crassness. The difference between overweening crassness and simple crassness is easily identified. The latter is an infringement of so-called normal conduct due to inadvertence or disorientation in worldly affairs, or the affairs of this world. Overweening crassness is exceeding the bounds of normality in a programmatic way, in order to display one's superiority and super-orientation in worldly affairs. Simple crassness is refusing to walk two hundred metres from the parking lot. Overweening crassness is advertising this fact with one's horn and using it as outward testimony to one's own power.

Crassness in the psychological sense of the word exists without overweeningness. But overweeningness in the sociological sense of the word cannot exist without crassness.

Once in Spain a society for the protection of animals was founded which was hard up for money. They put on some large bullfights.
KURT TUCHOLSKY
1890-1935

Boundary Burning

A little old man used to live near us, Jungmann was his name, and he was dreadfully fond of burning field boundaries. As soon as nature dried out a little and licked itself from its winter snows, there he was with his matches and thick clouds of smoke wreathed the fallow fields and villages. The little old man reckoned burning the boundaries was the best boost for nature as it licked itself from its winter snows. Disliking theories and newfangled ways, he regarded artificial fertiliser as the scourge of the Lord and talk of natural balance as slanderous to common sense, something with which in his declining years he was filled to overflowing. I do not know why so much common sense is acquired in one's declining years, probably it is because one has more time and human nature centres upon those functions which still remain to it. And acts of reason are that much more difficult to evaluate than muscular strength.

That little old man Jungmann simply reckoned that ash was the best fertiliser, that all insects and worms were harmful and birds were the worst nibblers of crops. In botany he reckoned only with potatoes, in zoology with cows. And he rendered up burnt offerings to approaching spring, as though it were a precondition for the victory of spirit over matter.

It was not easy to discuss things with him. One was hampered by his reverend grey hairs, by his rather less reverent diction and his habit of using a stick or fork as a syntactic crutch. It was necessary nevertheless to do something about this burning of boundaries, for supra-local organs were by now animadverting to it. Thus there arose the set ceremonial of criticising little old Jungmann for his boundary burning. As soon as the grass blazed up, one of the local dignitaries would appear according to a pre-arranged list, locate the old man joyfully cavorting amid the smoke and from a certain distance cite the strictures of the law concerning the burning of boundaries, maintenance of order in public places and the wreathing of fallow fields and communities in smoke. Initially the little old man defended himself stoutly against all criticism, and this gave rise to a certain amount of cross-country running practice, but later on he got used to it. He would hear out the criticism, nod his grey-haired head and depart to kindle another boundary. A record was nevertheless kept of the fact that the criticism of the burning had been carried out and the citizenry admonished accordingly.

So it came about that through this criticism little old Jungmann's boundary burning was in some sense legally sanctioned, and the old man began positively to welcome it, for by it he gained a relatively powerful argument against his smoke-infested neighbours. Ah yes, the man would say, I've spoken to the councillor about it. And there the matter rested. The boundaries went on being burnt and the criticism went on being administered.

I cannot think why I have just recollected these criticisms of little old Jungmann. Maybe it's because it reminds me of the carrying out of other such criticisms and communal chastisements. And maybe it's because I want to say, rather old Jungmann than more of that kind of criticism. One day those bumble-bees will be back.

The Scent of Illusions

Illusion, classed by many experts among the amaranths, but numbered by those too fond of gloom among the hemlocks, smells most pungent in its last phase of bloom.
KAREL KONRÁD
1960

62

> **Everything has been said already.**
> **But not everyone has said it.**
> STANISŁAW JERZY LEC
> 1964

Already the Ancient Sumerians

As palaeoanthropological investigation discovers more and more new and ever more ancient forerunners of the apes and human beings, and as archaeological discovery advances further and further into greater millenia B.C. and more and more cultures emerge out of the mists of time, so we get the impression (whether optimistic or pessimistic, I am unable to say), that it's all sort of happened before, our bodies and souls are somehow much older than we thought, and we are much more ancient and so relatively, in view of this great age, less perfect. And less wise.

Archaeology today represents the largest and most successful area of popularising literature, and this is certainly due not only to the chance supply of capable authors, but also to the interest of the consumer. We thus acquire the impression that already the ancient Sumerians (say possessed a system of school education remarkably similar to ours), and already the ancient Etruscans (manufactured modern vases)...Not to mention myths, organisation of warfare and administration and other less palpable phenomena.

It seems, nevertheless, that given this nourishing and tasty archaeological diet we fall victim to a certain optical illusion, precisely to do with this 'it's all happened before'. There were remarkable cultural achievements, there was astonishing theoretical learning, there was ungraspable graspable aesthetic feeling, but there was not the absolutely fundamental material level of civilisation or broader human base, capable of maintaining not only the tender flowers of cultures, but also the stability of ethnic and social cohesion in the face of onslaughts of natural adversity and rampant barbarism. There were remarkable intellectual achievements, enabled amongst other things by a scarcely imaginable process of eugenic selection, which modern society, guaranteeing the survival and reinforcement of even genetically less resilient factors and individuals, simply will not and cannot allow. But there was no broader human base to reflect the intellectual achievements, maintain them as biological factors, and apply them in practice.

And so it seems to me that in comparing ourselves with the Sumerians we are not comparing like with like. We are comparing the song of the nightingale with a score for symphony orchestra.

Spiritual achievements are in a way merely a mechanism of adaptation to the material state of the world, the given human world, they are an ever recurrent effort to search for some point d'appui in space and time, nature and history, which is of course less shaped by these achievements than we would like. They are the reflection of acts, but they are not acts in themselves. Though they get to the roots they are not the roots.

And so in going back to the Sumerians and discovering those amazing cultural affinities, we should perhaps cast suspicion rather upon our own cultural achievements and organisational principles as being possibly antiquated. For – if Sumerian schools were good enough for the Sumerians, they are probably not quite good enough for us. For, as Brecht says, if it is like that, it cannot be left like that.

...He only believes in thought transference,
because he's been lying in bed for twenty years...
BOHUMIL HRABAL
1969

On Supernatural Forces

Even the most enlightened individual, one who fundamentally, consciously, and on principle rejects all form of metaphysical crutch, now and then allows himself to get carried away by two sorts of illusion. The first is that 'it'll all work out in the end', in other words, there's no point in agonising over any terribly detailed plan of action or intervention, for things have a way of falling into place by themselves, and you only have to give them a little shove, randomly, now and again. Eloquent witness to just such a faith in the supernatural automatism of things is the little boy who, having squeezed the contents of a toothpaste tube out on to the floor, and being summoned to his supper, declares: Yes, I'm coming, soon as I get the toothpaste back in the tube! It may perhaps be good now and again to look about of an evening and guess at the amount of toothpaste lying around which, in our supernatural optimism, we believe capable of being restored to its original status. After a while such an inspection will convince us that toothpaste and all other like objects are governed exclusively by physical laws. One hazardous variant of the belief that everything will work out all right in the end is to rely on someone else solving matters for us. Or else on nobody ever noticing. In this sense the factory which emits toxic waste into a river and pollutes five square kilometres of countryside must be considered a particularly lethal version of the little boy with the toothpaste tube.

The second illusion which seizes upon the individual is a belief in the supernatural spark. Slumbering genius. Though buried in the ashes of self-indulgence and apathy, we still believe in the strict privacy of our own souls that the Phoenix lies dormant within us, ready to rise up any moment glowing with an historic fire. Experience shows of course, that practically nothing ever rises from the ashes, except perhaps an ash-strewn chicken. Insofar as anything fiery ever does materialise, it is never the result of waiting, but of about two to three decades (or in quite exceptional cases say half a decade) of effort, deliberate slog and exhaustive will power. "Supernatural" forces and acts are liberated and elicited only by the most natural of ways and means.

The foundation of reasoned optimism in life is the awareness that in most situations it depends entirely on us, the participants, how things turn out, and that every tiny spark within us requires a thorough pumping of the bellows.

The essence of belief is the establishment of a habit.
CHARLES SANTIAGO SANDERS PIERCE
1839-1914

The Magnetic Amulet

According to the calendar the medieval age is long behind us, but I cannot shake off the impression that with its tiny feelers and spindly legs it still, from a distance, participates in the moulding of protoplasma into concrete human forms: a notable result of this participation is the amulet of protection against disease. Of course it is no longer the heart of a cat killed in the new moon by boiling in gherkin brine, nor minced asses' droppings nor the laces of a hanged man's topboots. It is not carried in a little bag of sackcloth in one's bodice. It is neither charmed nor consecrated, nor is it supplied with runes and pentacles, and there is no obligation upon acquiring it to spit thrice over one's left shoulder.

It is a chic bangle, gold-tinged in hue, of Japanese manufacture and obtainable at Tuzex hard-currency shops, insofar as not yet replaced by a cooperative domestic product of the same ilk. It suffices to encircle one's left wrist with it and without further ceremonial, by mere diurnal and nocturnal wearing of the object, one obtains protection against various ailments, such as headaches, lumbago, rheumatoid pains termed a touch of the rheumatics, kidney stone colics, erysipelas and doubtless also the falling sickness and the Black Death.

The secret of its effectiveness is neither the will of Vishnu nor of Ammon, but – in view of the scientific spirit of the age – magnetism.

And what effectiveness this is! This amulet is said to be two and a half to three times more powerful than a visit to your health clinic and to vie even with analgesics, while being de facto cheaper when taken over an eight-month period.

Yet enough of these frivolous words: already I see the fists flashing in the balmy early summer breeze, I see the threatening glints of the bangles on everyone's wrists. Yes, the magnetic bangle has helped you and us too. I gladly believe it. Once in his day a renowned Czech urologist gave patients of his suffering from stones in their urinary tracts a special medicine supplied with a mysterious inscription and strictly personalised instructions for use. The results of the treatment were astonishing. It was simply pure re-distilled water, but nobody knew that.

And in that lies the undeniable positive feature of such medicines: at least they harm nobody, while having only one single side effect: simple sincere faith. Would that other more well-qualified factors in our lives and environment might awaken it also.

> **Most human beings have an almost infinite capacity for taking things for granted.**
> ALDOUS HUXLEY
> 1894-1963

The Head-Capping Principle

By the head-capping principle we mean that phenomenon whereby all (respectable) persons, man or boy, regardless of the prevailing weather with the exception of heatwaves, consider it essential to cover their heads whenever leaving their place of habitation. Neighbour K.E. does this, in spite of the fact that he is saving on heating and the temperature at home is lower than it is outside. Neighbour K.E. is a wise and well-informed man, for he reads the Sunday supplements, and therefore believes that if we fail to cover our heads 1. we catch a draught, 2. we get a cold in the brain, 3. we get inflammation of the middle ear, 4. our hair drops out, 5. we become complete imbeciles. On being asked what catching a draught means, he declares himself unable to say exactly, but some doctor or other was writing about it only the other day, and he knows. Neighbour K.E.'s views on the importance of keeping one's head covered are shared by an absolute majority of my neighbours, even though they are unaware of the doctor who wrote something about draughts just recently. On the other hand we have never met any dermatologist familiar with the fatal correlation between hair falling out and not wearing headgear, nor do we know of any neurologist who could explain why a healthy head, unafflicted by any ailment of the respiratory passages or sinuses, should need some object placed upon it. In frost for example the less well-guarded extremities such as the nose and ear-lobes have rather more evident need of protection than the more or less hirsute vaults of the scalp.

Nevertheless these neighbours, though fit as a fiddle, all place on their heads with neurotic care exceedingly comic objects such as Cossack caps, Indian fur hats, Russian fur caps, perforated hats, Sherlock-Holmesian check caps, or woolly hats at the very least. The last two varieties are of course worn only by persons less concerned for their dignity, one-off characters indeed. Covering their heads they deem they have done sufficient to ensure the health of body, mind and hair.

I am unable to fathom the reason for this principle. Perhaps there exists some fifth law of thermodynamics, which my teachers concealed from me. Perhaps some primitive ancient man was sent by the appropriate agency into the world with the command – go forth and multiply, but don't forget to take your hat. Perhaps there exists some male brotherhood of worthy fighters, whose initiation ceremony consists of the fitting on of a hat, and whose members are obliged on pain of death to wear their head markings everywhere and always, even if beneath the fur hat they have the look of a bream with a tortoise on top.

In any event the head-capping principle teaches us that in this life there are many fixed and reliable persistent procedures which it is unwise to breach. An individual neglecting such principles exposes himself to stigma and suspicion. If only for the reason that he finds himself unable to doff his cap at the appropriate juncture.

He who lacks temperament
must look for ornament.
KARL KRAUS
1874-1936

For Beauty and Health

I know not what it is, but legal advice in the press is offered by lawyers, whereas health advice is offered by anyone, relying as a rule on age-old folk wisdom, for our ancestors were somehow simply healthy. Except that they died.

Neighbour K.E., famed for his learning obtained by reading of the Sunday supplements, determined to make use of the benefits of water cure, fervently promoted therein. He began with a glass of lukewarm water taken in the morning on an empty stomach, for this settles the digestion and enhances the skin. His skin was in no way affected, but it regulated his digestion magnificently, for after the lukewarm water he would regularly vomit and be unable to eat until the afternoon. After he withdrew from this internal hydropathic treatment the habit remained of preferring not to eat in the morning.

Other advice neighbour K.E. was able to implement only in part. This was for instance alternate hot and cold showers, which refresh everyone and revive the circulation, as well as making smokers' blood vessels more resistant to toxic nicotine. Showers may be augmented

with bathing the upper half of the body in cold water, to which many a woman owes her firm and lovely bust. Wisely enough neighbour K.E. ignored the latter item and went for the showers. As an inveterate chain-smoker he adapted some advice from a Do-It-Yourself column and devised a small but nifty cigarette shelter for using under the shower; it was made of PVC and fixed to some motorist's goggles. The cigarettes were thus safely protected and neighbour K.E. continued with the hot and cold showers until such time as he suffered a heart attack and had to go to the clinic. So that the nicotine-resistant vessels maybe had not enough time to form.

But he placed his highest hopes in bathing for 15 minutes in water up to 39°C, into which one may add an infusion of camomile, lavender, and even peppermint, alternatively a mug of milk or buttermilk, and the effect of the bath may be enhanced by drinking at the same time a cup containing 'an infusion of the listed active ingredients'. Neighbour K.E. began with the mint, and when he had swallowed the required cupful he suddenly came over so peculiar, that once he had summoned aid and crawled out of the bath he felt indeed like a new-born babe. He recovered however in a couple of days and tried it with milk, although other neighbours advised cream in preference, arguing that our forebears would've been unable to afford it, whereas we could, and that included neighbour K.E. After eight milky immersions the bath was so dirty that various algae and moulds were growing in it, which K.E. stubbornly considers part of the whole curative effect and refuses to remove.

A cock to Aesculapius! Neighbour K.E. is just as healthy and unhealthy as he was before his water cure, a shining example of how even the derring-do of universal health advice may be surmounted.

The shortest distance between two points
is not always a straight line.
NIKOLAY LOBACHEVSKY
1792-1856

In order to be yourself you first have to be somebody.
STANISŁAW JERZY LEC
1964

The Laws of Being and Representing

One really serious problem in life is how not only to be something, but also to represent it. In a very particular, specialised form this problem occurs in the realm of film art. In film (for example) it is not simply a matter of being young or being a grower of aubergines, it is a matter of how to make manifest this state in some way or other. To show it as it were in action. With growers of aubergines it is relatively easy, the subject is simply surrounded with aubergines, aubergines poke out of his pockets and conversation turns to the subject of artificial fertiliser. With youth it is much more complicated. Youth does not poke out of pockets and does not reveal itself in any evident way in speech, or at least, when it does, not in a form appropriate for the film medium.

For this reason the young spend a lot of time in films running about. No proper young person in films these days just walks along, he runs, and if there is the slightest pretext, he absolutely sprints, without getting out of breath of course, all most effective, especially with female figures, who sprint along winsomely and lightly, dressed in a suitable get-up. If the young are to display love, their readiness to make short dashes, or even cross-country runs, is notably increased. The enamoured young run especially in forests and on the banks of picturesque waters, while the girl takes delight in catching hold of tree-trunks and rotating around them; subsequently she is caught up with by her partner, embraced, and then the camera cuts to another scene. Very strong emotion is emphasised in running by whooping sounds, which in no way disturb the regularity of breathing. Any young man in a film who does not run probably has problems, serious and just ones, if he is a positive figure. If corrupted youth is the theme, it hardly ever runs, but props up walls round corners, smokes fags and plots nastiness.

With scientific types it is quite different. The film scientist demonstrates his scientific outlook by incorrigible bookishness. On the domestic scene he has books everywhere. On opening a book he instantly orientates himself and quotes passages. The absent-minded boffin may search in vain for socks or his key, but never a book. The young scientist is full of sweeping locks of hair and bold plans for the future. His books are thinner in bulk, but he is instantly orientated too. Apart from books the proper scientific type has a home laboratory, for clarity's sake usually all mixed up with the books. The laboratory comprises a multitude of jars and retorts, whose contents are decanted with emissions of smoke and dark colours, in the case of serious or hazardous experiments. The laboratory of a positive scientist figure usually has something purloined from it by a suitable scoundrel, who has smoothly combed hair, a colourful tie and a perfectly fitting suit. During the action he smokes, and if a particularly dangerous specimen, smokes cigars.

Technicians are marked by having large drawing boards, on which they are always just finishing something, never just starting, always just completing, and it always continues late on into the night, disturbing their matrimonial or neighbourly relations. Young technicians generally have a mistake somewhere in their drawings, but this is remedied before the conclusion.

Those are just remarks at random, to demonstrate something of the laws of representative being.

This attempt to be saved by the hue and cry of the age
reminds me of the forthrightness of some journalist
who wanted the Czech king George of Poděbrady
mounted on the equestrian statue of a Habsburg emperor.

VLADISLAV VANČURA
1891-1942

The Laws of Representing and Being

We have indicated how conventionally to represent what one is, using the special case of film. This is of course an artistic procedure.

Matters get more complex however when we realise that in films it is not enough to be even simply a child in order successfully to represent a child. For this reason special hunts are laid on to search for suitable filmogenic children. A child in a film is not simply itself, but has to demonstrate itself clearly, something which is achieved 1. by open-air frolickings, even though outside the film world such children's frolickings are never to be seen; 2. ball-games, in particularly realistic films football with two sets of goalposts, where all the actors have to yell 'pass' or 'over here', even though in real life such football pitch calls are never to be heard, for they are replaced by others, probably cinematographically inappropriate; 3. tireless activity in a domestic setting, usually quite spacious, where furniture is shifted around in a jocular manner and people are tied up with washing lines, for playing in films usually consists of cowboys and Indians. A child playing say at being a rabbit and sitting still for that reason in a sideboard like a toadstool, as I myself was wont blithely to do, is cinematographically unsuitable. Nor did I ever act as a child in a film. In film the child who simply squats around is usable only as evidence of a broken home.

It follows from this, that representing may, or must at times be distinguished clearly from being. In films for example. But also in other cases. Take for instance the Black-Throated Diver Breeders' Society. This Society, as its statutes prescribe, holds an annual general meeting together with a tombola and cultural programme. Due to a severe shortage of black-throated divers the members of the Society cannot breed any, they are merely potential black-throated diver breeders and as such represent themselves both to themselves and to the rest of the world through their annual general meeting, tombola and cultural programme. Without the general meeting there would be no question of having any black-throated divers, of which there are none anyway, but if there were no general meeting there would be none even de jure, which would certainly be a serious infringement of the natural equilibrium. The members of the Black-Throated Diver Breeders' Society are thus an example of representing not only preceding but even replacing being. And lo, they find it all perfectly acceptable. The same goes for neighbour L.K., who is, let us call it, a high-tension air-conditioning technician, represented in his case by a characteristic bag slung over his shoulder. High-tension air-conditioning technology either does not exist, or does not function, there being no spare parts available, but neighbour L.K. with the aid of his bag represents its state of apparent being. And lo, he finds it all quite acceptable.

And so it often appears that representing is more important than being. And this in turn is represented as being perfectly acceptable.

Art is the spiritual life, made possible by science.
W.H. AUDEN
1959

How We Were Filmed

It was agreed that a sequence would be shot of the laboratory, with us doing something to do with mice. The laboratory and the mouse were at the ready. The film people arrived. On seeing the laboratory and the mouse they went visibly glum.

– Haven't you got the odd retort at least? they enquired.

– Or one or two glass tubes with something running about inside?

– Or something on a Bunsen burner, bubbling away and letting off steam?

– And the mouse is that small and ugly? Shyly we explained that we had neither retorts nor steam, nor mice of better appearance, and yet we did do experiments, without even lighting a Bunsen burner.

– Yes, said the cameraman, but like this it doesn't look at all like science! It looks just like an ordinary room. Couldn't you get in a big microscope or a telescope or something?

We couldn't. The film people unpacked their stuff with distaste and lit up the mouse and the hand which was to give it an injection.

– How do you give it an injection? they asked. We showed them.

– But we can't do a close-up of that, it would make people sick, the producer said, evidently feeling a little sick already.

Then they sat us down in front of some small bits of apparatus ready to hand and asked us all together to do some looking through microscopes, measuring of pHs, spinning in centrifuges, weighing on scales, drawing through pipettes and taking of records, waving our hands about abundantly the while, so as to put a bit of life in it (the life of science). The cameraman also lit a Bunsen burner for the purpose.

Reflecting on what was typical and what was atypical, and how you wave your hands about in the course of scientific endeavour, we entered into our parts and the camera started to roll. Meantime the film assistants opened up the cage of mice, which scampered nimbly off across the tables. In the ensuing melee the cameraman knocked over the Bunsen burner, setting some documents on fire, and while this was being put out a cylinder of pipettes fell over shattering with a joyful crash into tiny smithereens. The mice gambolled about as if in a circus, the microscopes softly glowed, and delicately purple haematoxylin trickled across the table.

– That's more like it, the cameraman exclaimed, joyfully overturning a container of pH 7,4 saline solution.

– Now it's got a bit more life in it, see, remarked the producer at the end of the take, relatively satisfied.

– Right, and now the whole thing all over again, and give it all you've got, he appended.

We said no. They had to make do with the lifeless shots they already had. They left totally disenchanted. This science stuff just doesn't look like science. What does?

> **In the future, everyone will be famous for 15 minutes.**
> ANDY WARHOL
> 1965

The Metaphysics of Photography

One may see it in Czechoslovakia, but even more anywhere in the world. One may see it at events both glorious and inglorious, in joy and in sadness, at times of splendour and times of calamity. One may see: that while people single or in their thousands are marching, fleeing, wondering in amazement, standing to attention, clam-

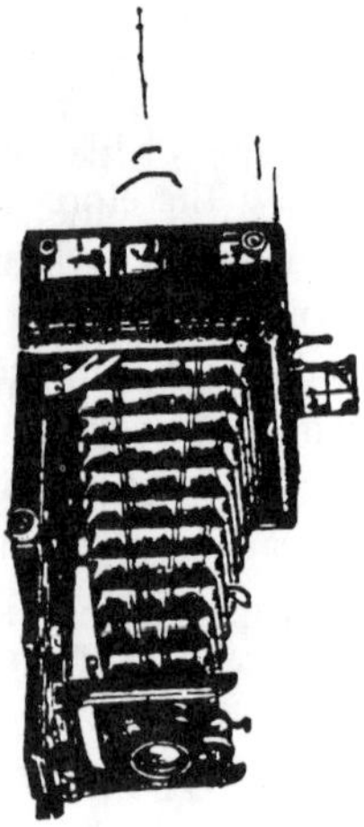

ouring, keeping mum, or clinging with their gazes, hands or thoughts to the events in question, one person is neither marching nor fleeing, nor standing to attention, neither clamouring nor keeping mum, but clicking, walking against the flow or standing within the flow, and not clinging on to the action, but moving about in the middle or round the perimeter of the said event. He is there to evaluate the said event and record it, and therefore arrogates to himself a kind of unearthly sanctitude. Or indeed enjoys some kind of unearthly sanctitude. He is, of course, a photographer.

I used to believe quite mistakenly that in order to run about during the national anthem, push one's way through to a fire, climb over police barricades and wade in a tank of killer whales, one needed authorisation, some kind of paper and permit, albeit kept hidden in the pocket. It is not so. The camera is quite sufficient, along with the determination to photograph. In many, if not all situations at least. If we want to get nearer an active volcano than others, it is enough to take out a camera and adopt the intention. If we wish to scamper around during a funeral or make our way comparatively unscathed against the current of hordes of people rushing along with either good or evil intent, all we have to do is wave a camera and look constantly through the viewfinder.

The camera is one of those few fruits of civilisation that enables one for a moment to step outside the flux of action and be otherwise and elsewhere. The camera is a kind of time machine accessible to all. And it has nothing at all to do with the results of the photographic endeavour, whoever could ever bear to spend more than ten minutes looking at the slides of us amateur photographers. It is a matter of the act of photographing itself, its psychology. In peaceful, so to speak leisure activities the camera in the hands of an amateur may be a disturbing element, preventing the user from being and living in pleasure. In exceptional situations however it becomes a metaphysical instrument, a means of transcending human reactions and mass movements. During a tornado at Wichita Falls in Texas a number of house-owners with cameras ready to hand stopped running away and started filming. Nothing happened to them. During the crash of a DC 10 at Chicago airport one bystander stopped staring and photographed the plane as it began to fall out of the sky, in spite of the fact that it was heading straight for him. It missed.

I judge therefore, that in the Great Deluge somebody will be found with a camera ready to hand and he will be the dove. And at the Last Judgment a photographer will run about with an exposure meter measuring the light on the face of the Lord in his fury. And hence will be saved, evading final judgment.

And so I keep my camera respectfully ever at the ready.

> **The trouble with the world is that the stupid are cocksure and the intelligent are full of doubt.**
>
> BERTRAND RUSSELL
> 1872-1970

The Art of Conversation

Some arts are developed and perfected, only to shrink and decay again in the fullness of time. One of these is the art of conversation, meaning conversation as conducted in our mass media, which, in my judgment, ought to be not only a means to imparting learning and information, but also a school of lively wit and good taste.

At the moment this art is for us definitely in its decadent stage. All too many interviewers and presenters possess the following sort of arsenal of artful questions:

1/ So – um – what could you say to listeners by way of introduction? (Here follows a response introduced as a rule by words such as Well, Yes, or the genial phrase Yes, absolutely right, Mr Presenter…)

2/ Would you like to add something to this (alternatively: what you have just said)?

(Here follows the second part of the response, usually fairly similar to the first.)

3/ Is there anything you would like to add by way of conclusion?

(Here follows the same as we had at the beginning, but in slightly different words and garnished with warm familiarities.)

Discussions (or chat shows) introduced like this and improvised with such striking forethought can of course scarcely provide any great feastings of the spirit.

The kindergarten of taste gets its final bodyblow in those chats with popular personalities enjoying universal respect, whom the presenter resolves to address as familiarly as possible, perhaps in order to evidence his intimate relations with the being in question. A chat with Albert Einstein comes out something like this:

PRESENTER: Well now, Berty, we'd all like to welcome you on the programme and we're just so very glad you could make it over tonight.

EINSTEIN: (takes a sip of something and utters a few remarks about the special theory of relativity, but is interrupted.)

PRESENTER: Quite so, Bert, great stuff. But now I'm sure our listeners (viewers) would appreciate maybe um something a bit lighter. Did anything funny at all happen to you during all this?

EINSTEIN: (painfully cobbles together a funny story, mostly far less entertaining than the theory of relativity itself, but is interrupted before he reaches the punch line.)

PRESENTER: Hah, hah. Well that's really...But unfortunately, listeners, our time is now up, so in conclusion I – it only remains for me to say that next week we're having our old friend Vanya Pavlov along...(Without further ado the set goes dark in front of a fidgety Einstein.)

I suppose these masters of conversation also rant on sometimes about our lack of social decorum.

In the most primitive societies – if one believes the anthropologists – the principal function of ritual, religion, of culture as it is practised is, in fact, almost to stop change. It is to provide for the social organism what life provides in such a magic way for living organisms, a kind of homeostasis... Today culture and tradition have assumed a very different intellectual and social purpose; ...the principal function of the most vital and living traditions today is precisely to provide the instruments of rapid change.

J. ROBERT OPPENHEIMER
1959

The Computer Serial

The American firm Sunn Classic makes family entertainment programmes for TV, and there is certainly nothing odd about that. Family entertainment programmes are made by many firms, and many of the firms and individuals involved have to compensate for limitations of a professional and technical nature by exerting artistic abilities, whether real or supposed. The special thing about Sunn Classic is that it bases its work on computer automation. The President of Sunn Classic is forty-year-old Charles Seiler, a computer specialist.

So the firm collects the basic demographic data, especially the interests and proclivities of the envisaged consumers, and feeds them into a computer along with the construction principles of the required script. The computer then sketches out a story. Thus for example Sunn Classic discovered that the public loves waterfalls, pretty landscapes, mountain crags, the free and even downright wild life of nature. Landscape scenes are more attractive if actors and animals are dispersed over them. The public is not over-fond of snow, except in relation to Christmas. The public prefers permanent natural ice, amidst which a pleasantly rough but emotion-packed storyline unfolds. There need not be any women, we've had enough of them already. Better are manly feelings and relationships. Let tension alternate with tenderness and let the ending be reconciliatory if not downright happy. These overall data are composed by the computer down to the last blade of grass and breath of zephyr. And so there arose the first computer television serial called Grizzly Adams, a loving and warm story of love between a rough mountain dweller and an even rougher grizzly bear. Of course

Seiler has to devote much more time and money to researching and preparing the script than he does to its actual realisation, but on the other hand he ensures virtually certain consumer success for his product. Nothing is left to chance and so-called intuition, certainty is the name of the game. In the future according to Seiler the industry will have no room for the individual scriptwriter who contributes a story however marvellous. The first priority will be not the writer, but the demographic data, potential audience and currently preferred assembly of images and plots. All of which will be accurately processed by the computer.

To the romantic way of thinking this naturally sounds repellent. To this way of thinking the very notions of industrial production and the mass media are of course repellent. This attitude refuses to recognise that a person is equally influenced, even ruled, by industry, in terms of taste in dress and adornment, from jeans to haircuts. So that this represents only a little bit more, a little bit of screen-gazing. The problem is of course what kind of slide this automated computer regulation would induce in consumer taste itself. So that even in an age of computer serials flattering our taste-buds, art will still be needed.

> **All people are actors,**
> **but where do we find them a repertoire?**
> STANISŁAW JERZY LEC
> 1964

Mickey Mouse from the Biological Point of View

In 1978 Mickey Mouse was fifty years old. In the course of the years the size of his eyes grew from 27% of the length of his head to 42%. The length of his head grew from 42.7% of the length of his body to 48.1%. The frontal arching of the head grew through backward shifting of the ears by about 28%. Note that large heads, large eyes and frontal arching are signs of infantility, likewise short legs and arms, also made more prominent in Mickey's case. Mickey Mouse has developmentally regressed. This anatomical change has been accompanied by a corresponding psychological alteration; the somewhat sadistic, wicked and reckless Mouse of the 1930s has become such a nice decent little fellow that in 1953 Mickey out fishing was unable to deal with even a mischievous shellfish.

This is no accident, says the biologist and essayist S. J. Gould, who has measured the Mouse's proportions with scientific precision. Disney's cartoonists discovered, probably unwittingly, that the signs of infantility listed above awaken irresistible sympathy and positive protective feeling within us. These are the features in little bunny rabbits, puppies, kittens and fledglings which make us find them so delightful, projecting on to them the emotional attachment designed for our own young. Irresistible sympathy is understandably good for box-office receipts. Commercial success was thus the developmental factor transforming Mickey to the point where he became – biologically speaking – neotenic, that is, showing progressive retention of immature characteristics at a certain late stage of growth over successive generations.

The anatomical development of Mickey Mouse even recapitulates our own evolutionary history. For human beings are likewise somewhat neotenic. People retain into adulthood features which were positively infantile in our ancestors. Australopithecus stood in the same relation to us as Mickey of the thirties to Mickey of the fifties. Adult persons are less different from their embryos than adult chimpanzees are. If primates in general may be distinguished from other mammals by their perceptible developmental retardation in individuals, we have taken things so far that our embryonic development, including increase in brain size, persists into the period following birth, and the absolute and relative length of our childhood is incomparably greater than that of any other animal. The consequences in terms of adaptability, educability and transfer of cultural values are obvious. As Konrad Lorenz wrote: 'That characteristic of a real person so essential for human features – the prolonged period of remaining in a state of development – is quite certainly a gift which we owe to the neotenic quality of the human race.'

The only thing we still lack compared to Mickey Mouse is that state of being a nice decent little fellow. In that sense the Mouse is still quite a little way ahead of us.

Si necessitatis est, peccatum non est;
si voluntatis, vitari potest.
If it is a necessity, then it is not a sin;
if it is optional, then it can be avoided.
PELAGIUS
ca 360 - *ca* 420

The Visitant

Villains arrive when all seems fine and the room presents a peaceful interior; only the ticking of the clock is perhaps noticeably loud. Heroes turn up just when it seems evil is about to triumph and the innocent victims are on their last gasp. But neither of these is the kind of visitant I have in mind.

The kind I have in mind is that totally benign, otherwise ill-definable visitant who turns the doorhandle just when you are counting up in your head an enormous long list of five figure numbers, you are on the hundreds, the sub-total is ninety-eight, and you are muttering this to yourself under your breath: he softly arrives, greets you politely, and says in a totally unassuming voice: Excuse me, would you mind telling me the time?

Alternatively he arrives at a moment of fatal parting, ne'er again, your breath is tense, your heart seethes (with bitterness and so on), you are hanging on her (his) lips, and now he enters, trips modestly over the threshold and says in a totally unassuming voice: Sorry…um…to interrupt, but could I have left my brolly here?

Whereupon he spends the rest of his visit and your time searching for it. Or else he arrives just when both of your telephones are ringing, the report on your last and next twenty years' work has to be completed and submitted in the next two minutes, some papers have caught fire in the wastepaper bin, something has bust in the centrifuge, and there are eight other people in the room already; he arrives and says (very gently) in a totally unassuming voice: Hello, old chap, look, will you be interested in any of this year's narcissi?

Or finally, he makes his appearance just when the building is being evacuated due to fire, whitewashing or mass evacuation drill, he threads his way through the throngs all hurtling the other way, opens the door of the room where one has just nipped back to fetch the last of one's odds and ends, and says, in a totally unassuming voice: Hi, it's me, have you got a moment to spare?

He is an unheroic, innocent visitant. Humble and patient. Quiet and devoted. Irreproachable. Even though we may suspect he provided the original pretext for cannibalism.

Extensive study of the subject has led me to the belief that this innocent form of visitation demands enormous talent. The gift of the gods, those whose job it is to subject human kind to the sternest of trials. This visitant's talent consists in always selecting the best moment to strike, without ever skulking villain-like behind doors or being summoned like a conquering hero. It lies also in the pure dedication with which he steps onward through life towards further undeserved rebuffals. And lastly, no small talent is required to choose the topics to be raised and cultivated by this unwitting exterminating angel, whenever the times rage furiously out of joint.

He is omnipresent, ever alert, the genius of our everyday dramas, the touchstone of the operation of our central nervous system, and ...Sorry, someone has just turned up.

And he said again: 'These are people coming afresh into the world (not knowing themselves from whence), nor yet do they know themselves, or that they are people: for there is darkness and nothingness about them, only a little shrieking and weeping. But when they walk along this street, slowly day breaks and dawns, till now they reach unto this gate beneath us: come, let us behold what here is afoot.'

JAN AMOS COMENIUS
The Labyrinth of the World, 1663

The Factor of First Encounter

Lopata Castle is first mentioned in 1377 as being in the hands of Hermann of Litice, and more recently in 1979, in Miroslav Horníček's book *In Praise of Outdoor Activity*, as the destination of an outing by the Czech Tourists Club. For these reasons I decided to use a visit to this castle as a means to instruct one small child C.H. on matters of historical fact. It is best to instruct children properly on all these matters of history.

We set off along the well-marked path through mixed woodland, into a clearing, across piles of signpost-ignoring logs and over slippery hillside leafage; each time I caught tumbling child C.H. just in time and used his tumble to explain how castles are always built in inaccessible, precipitous spots, variously blocked up or encumbered. On crossing some thoroughly rotting footbridge over a cavity in the ground I indicated the historic existence of an outer bailey formed by a pallisade and ditch. Then we arrived at the top of the hill, where, according to the guidebook, there used to be towers with walls 2.80 metres thick and 10 metres in diameter, two blocks of living quarters and massive stone walls, as well as the indispensible castle well. Now there were simply trees, two largish stones, one standing to a certain height, and a tablet announcing that the castle had come to grief in 1432, when that marauder Habart Maršík of Hrádek, besieged here by the Pilsner fencibles, was starved out, set the castle ablaze and fled by the back way. From then on evidently not very much had happened, only further visits by bands of Pilsners, leaving all too visible traces of touristy goings-on, especially in secluded nooks. I must say that neither the tablet, nor the two stones, in spite of their partly Gothic working, nor the cavity in the ground had a terribly impressive effect on the child. Having learned that for the first time in its life it was in a castle, it simply took this fact on board and demanded to be taken on the roundabouts.

What is worse, ever since this trip to Lopata Castle child C.H. is totally and unshakably convinced that a castle consists of two stones, a cavity in the ground, and...those all too visible traces of touristy goings-on. So that child C.H. now discovers castles all over the place, even in totally unhistoric urban and rural built-up areas, including bits of Prague's Charles Square. In the learning process child C.H. has succumbed to that undesirable deviation caused by the factor of first encounter, which is for human minds pretty well definitive.

The case of child C.H. is not dissimilar to that of a colleague of mine's grandmother; this old lady lived near the Sparta football club's Letná stadium, and she always refused to believe that 'those people were making such a dreadful racket' just because the ball had gone into the net. One day she was lured into the ground to see a real match with her own eyes, and the game went to a nil-nil draw. As a result Granny was never convinced of the sociological fact of a goal, and she continues to reckon they just do it on purpose so as to annoy the neighbours. Here too the factor of first encounter has led to a total conflict with reality.

It follows from this that we must choose our first encounters with great discretion, whether they be castles and marauding Habarts, or goals and contemporary chivalrous joustings. Or, come to that, secluded corners of Charles Square.

How Comes It That Lao-Tze Wrote a Book

'Those who speak know nothing;
Those who know are silent.'
These words, as I am told,
Were spoken by Lao-Tze.
If we are to believe that Lao-Tze
Was himself one who knew,
How comes it that he wrote a book
Of five thousand words?

PO-CHU-I
772-846

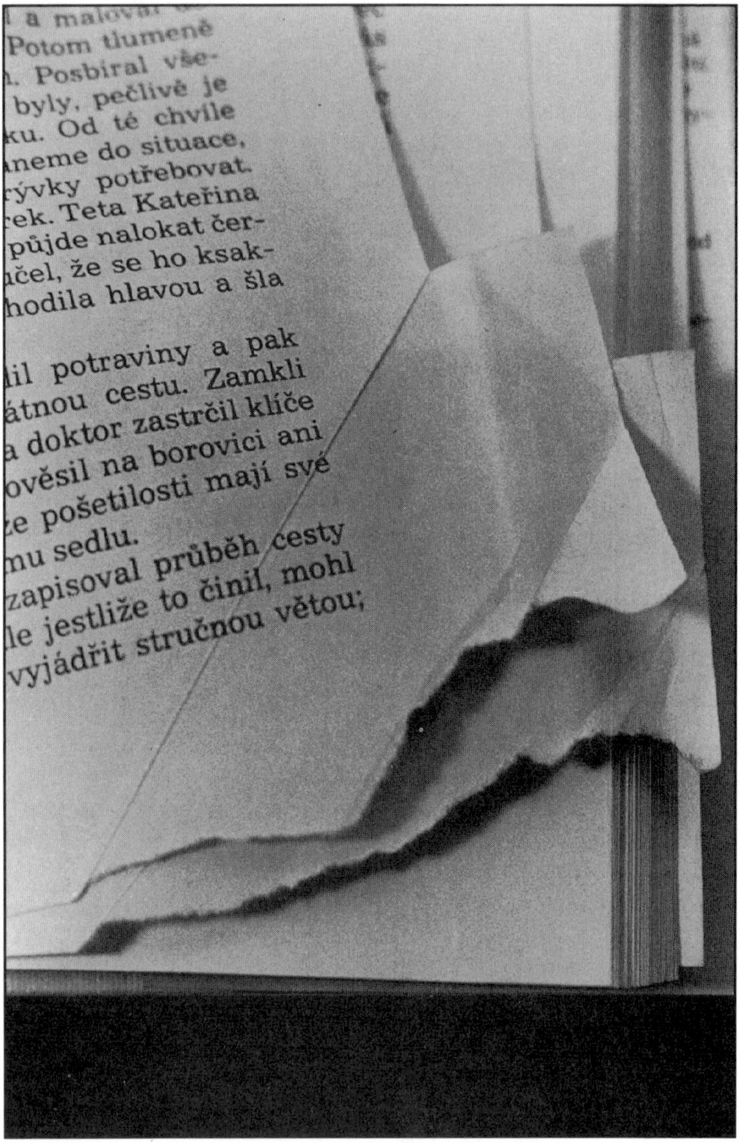
Potom tlumeně
. Posbíral vše-
byly, pečlivě je
ku. Od té chvíle
neme do situace,
rývky potřebovat.
ek. Teta Kateřina
půjde nalokat čer-
čel, že se ho ksak-
hodila hlavou a šla
il potraviny a pak
átnou cestu. Zamkli
a doktor zastrčil klíče
ověsil na borovici ani
ze pošetilosti mají své
mu sedlu.
zapisoval průběh cesty
le jestliže to činil, mohl
vyjádřit stručnou větou;

> ...the remainder of the people were busy with bells, mirrors, bladders, rattles and other trifles; some played even with their shadow, measuring, chasing, plucking it. All this so diligently, that many there were groaned and sweated, and some were overwrought by it.
> And almost everywhere were certain clerks or officers, who administered such things and distributed them with great devotion, while others there were hearkened with no less devotion unto them.
> And quoth I in wonderment: 'Alas, is man for this, that he should spend the sharpness of his heavenly wit upon such vain vile things?'
> 'Why vain?' quoth my interpreter. 'Is it not seen clear as in a mirror how, lo, these men o'ermaster all things with their wit? One does one thing, one another.'
> 'But all,' say I, 'not useful things, unfit for such a noble state of elevation.'
> 'Be not overwise,' said he again; 'for they are not in heaven yet; but on the earth must deal with earthly things. You see meanwhile, how properly everything goes forward.'
>
> JAN AMOS COMENIUS
> The Labyrinth of the World, 1663

The Treacherous Plumage of Words

Ideas, as far as there are any, have one terrible quality: they are hardly if at all transferable. Even the mere transference from so-called head to mouth is attended by such breaking, losing, binding, unbinding, darning, patching, sticking, tearing, picking, flapping, mending and padding, that the soaring eagle of thought is reduced to the moulting skin of a wren. I always receive with envy the statement that someone has formulated and expressed an idea. I have the idea, at least for my own part, that we ought to denote this otherwise. If what we think are ideas, then what we say are rather utterances. Articulations. And often blurtings. I do not claim that prior to transference every utterance existed as an idea. In many cases this possibility is virtually excluded. But that enormous quantity of utterances which we produce in a day suggests the probability that at least some of these somewhere and at some time or other existed as ideas. At the same time there is absolutely no guarantee that the suppression of utterances leads to a great flourishing of ideas. Silence, if golden, is often fool's gold. Ideas do not flourish, but come to a halt, for their stock is little depleted and a kind of negative feedback is induced. Transference from head to mouth appears to be essential more often than not.

But then comes that second transference, the transference of an utterance into an idea and utterance of another person. This is no longer mere tearing and darning, this is not the eagle turning into a little wren, but the corrosion, the fission of atoms, and the turning of the little wren into an antelope or other hoofed animal. Something all too familiar to anyone who has ever – as it is elegantly called – proffered an interview and then read what the other person wrote he allegedly said. Particularly good larkish fun occurs when interviews are proffered on the subject of science, but any other area of the interview-profferer's life will do for the purpose.

The unaccustomed profferer of interviews tends to suffer from after-shock, showing a neurotic tendency to complain and demand reparations, saying, for example, that he never said he had constant heart trouble after shock caused by personal ruin, but that his heart was troubled after finding Troska castle in ruins. When this emerges after further transference as a corrected statement saying that in spite of his poor health he founded a Society for the Preservation of Gothic Remains, the unaccustomed speaker collapses into a state of ruin himself and begins to suffer constant heart trouble. Whereas the accustomed speaker, aware of the problems of eagle transference, contents himself with any old hoofed animal, delighted that some of his utterances have accidentally begun to take on the semblance of real ideas.

In any case, there is no guarantee that, if without any process of transference our ideas could appear just as they occurred in the back of our mind, we would be any the wiser. More likely just more silent and more shivery with cold, in the absence of the cosy but treacherous plumage of words.

Joe Gould was the only man in the world who hit upon the idea that our history and our meaning might be best revealed *through* our talk.

WILLIAM SAROYAN

1963

On the Unnaturalness of Writing

Some people are so good at telling stories that the listener cannot help but say that one day he ought to write it all down. One of my friends spoke so grippingly about a Fourth League football match in his native hamlet that he deserved to be commissioned to write the national history of the sport. Another knows any amount about the illnesses of historic figures, such as Napoleon Bonaparte, who suffered such stomach and bladder trouble at the Battle of Waterloo that he was unable to devote himself properly to this world-shaping event, or the schizophrenia of Charles the Sixth, or the pernicious anaemia of the Valois family, he knows so much he could easily write a historical bestseller.

Another friend, whenever he comes to the laboratory, talks about the distribution of granules of ribonucleic acid in the cell and other intimate details of biology in such a revealing way that one absolutely longs to see his latest publication, but the quality is never there. It's not that he is inaccurate, but that when he sits down to write things get snarled up, extrapolations which are fine and charming in speech seem inadmissible in writing, his proposed theories unreasoned and premature, and so he ends up writing a conventional sober piece of work without any of the fireworks which he scatters exclusively by word of mouth.

Neither the football expert, who suffered a heart attack while playing table tennis, nor the historian, who suffers from a lack of time, want to write any of this down, and what they do write lacks both appeal and 'narrative claw', a term used by my Czech teacher, who of course never wrote anything either, with or without 'narrative claw'.

Between the ability to narrate and the ability to write narrative there seems to be a barrier such as few manage to cross. Those that do become writers, and they then start running out of topical narrative, so that they have to turn to the unaffected oral narrators in order to have anything to write about.

I reckon there is something very natural and innate about

story-telling, I reckon that while one primitive man painted the cave-walls of Lascaux, another sang to him and a third told stories, and that language in general was invented for story-telling, and not for the accumulation of information. That strange shyness that comes over us when we sit down to an empty sheet of paper is caused by this new, cold and demanding environment, for which neither we ourselves nor our languages are yet fully prepared. Story-telling is our talent, writing only a task imposed upon us by some collective perspective, a perspective so great that we are still a bit too small to live up to it. But what is art if not the repining of the little before the great.

Nevertheless, they still ought to write down all that stuff about football, about Charles the Sixth, and about the biochemistry of the cell.

Facts are ventriloquist's dummies.
Sitting on a wise man's knee they may be made to utter words of wisdom; elsewhere, they say nothing, or talk nonsense.
ALDOUS HUXLEY
1945

On the Naturalness of Speaking

In theory the basis of human speech is understanding, interpersonal communication, if possible influence. Let your words be judicious and contain the maximum of information. But try recording any old ordinary interpersonal conversation, or monologue conducted in the presence of others, on tape, and play it back at your leisure. You will find that even when you take the utmost care your speech is a heavily incoherent stream of clause fragments, scattered interjections, and various sub-lexical noises, pauses, loops and tangles. When we study an accurate transcript of our speech it turns out to be much thinner, much less dense in meaning than it seemed at the time, it is impoverished somewhow, downright incorrect in places and more often than not something is left out. What is left out is facial expression, gestures, position of head, position of hands, taking of breath, pausing and stressing through vocal quality, vocal intensity and vocal colouring. Whenever we try to concentrate fully on verbal expression, on verbal ordering and on the

target of our words, as a rule we start to be prolix, we start to duplicate and reiterate, we start in general to waffle a bit.

Some are better at speaking to the microphone than others, but in any case it is always quite different from when you have written it all down first. But then it is no longer simple speech, but a delivered speech, which loses a certain spontaneous charm. And sometimes meaning.

A particularly shocking experience is to tape-record a telephone conversation. Although gestures and grimaces do not have much of a role to play here, the recording contains a terrible number of reticences, hitches and extraneous noises, so that the whole thing recapitulated outside the telephone is so unwittingly absurd, pure verbal clowning, that the only person who can take it seriously is the other one with the telephone receiver to his ear who contributes to this acoustic carnival with apposite remarks such as Yes, Well there you are, You never, Well-in-my-case and so on: however, these observations from the other end of the line are absolutely essential, and when the other person falls silent he is urged on by questions such as Hello, you still there? to take a more active part in the communication.

It follows from this that our speech is influenced by our partners, situations and means of communication to such an extent that it is almost impossible to define it as verbal message per se, rather it is a very complex form of behaviour accompanied by verbal utterances, where the rest of the behaviour is, as often as not, rather more eloquent than the words themselves.

Hence comes the contrast between speaking and writing, where we have to substitute for the rest of the behaviour through more and different words, hence speech-making is physiologically speaking such a gruelling undertaking, and hence listening per se is such a harsh experience that as a rule we try to avoid doing it as much as possible.

Everything, in so far as it is in itself, endeavours to persist in its own being.

SPINOZA
1632-77

The Art of Non-Listening

The following type of conversational gambit is pretty familiar: 'Well now, that's enough chatting on about me, let's talk about you. How did you get on with my last book?'

I present this as an example of the self-absorbed person who wishes to hear of nothing but his own self.

Another fine type of conversational gambit is: 'Yes yes, so your oleander has flowered, you say? Now we happen to have a copy of Virgil's collected works signed by Pushkin. And Virgil you know, he once...' and so on and so forth, for ten minutes.

This is an example of the speaker who wishes to hear nothing but the sound of his own voice.

The gift of speech is usually taken to be something very individual. The gift of listening is much rarer, and notably inhibited by the former.

From which unfortunately it by no means necessarily follows that non-talkers are listeners, not to mention good listeners. Observation of non-talkers shows that while others speak they often sit with a glazed expression on their faces, not listening but reciting to themselves, silently, unshakeably and persistently 'But I...', 'But I...'

In all these cases one may suppose that non-listening acts as a sort of compensatory or defence mechanism to the speech of others.

I know however some remarkable types of non-listener in the primary and absolute sense. Such a one turns on the weather forecast, say, and as soon as the weather man gets to the area of low pressure over the Netherlands, he starts vociferously going on about once missing his train in Rotterdam and buying some yellow tulips; finally he declares how useless weather forecasts are these days. A hi-fi recording of the singer Karel Gott, of whom he is a great fan, is accompanied for such a one by a voluminous account of an encounter with the said singer somewhere in Prague. If he is at a lecture, even without a kindred soul within earshot, he utters at least for his own consumption some half-whispered dissenting remarks which enable him not to attend to what he is dissenting from. Without auditory stimuli from his surroundings however he usually maintains total silence.

This is the extreme type of pure non-listener and I would say that such behaviour is in fact instinctive. Something akin to the twittering of a bird induced by other twittering and intended to drown this other twittering. A twittering bird is probably basically happy; it just doesn't know what the weather is going to be. And maybe that's just why.

Distances are only the relation of space to time and vary with that relation.

MARCEL PROUST
1871-1922

The Principle of Crossed Letters

Letters as a literary form and as a means of communication between people are not in a flourishing state. Those times are gone when the correspondence of two persons famous in the eyes of others made up a whole book. Today even men of letters exchange mainly only factual missives, and only the letters of parents (or grandparents) to children (or grandchildren) occasionally contain a little narrative and wisdom in the spirit of that old song 'Mum she wrote to me today / Stray not from the sober way / Respect your officer my son...' Letters are non-flourishing to such an extent in fact that we cannot even talk of the exchange of letters any more. Rather we divide our friends, near and far, into those to whom we owe a letter ourselves, and those who owe a letter to us. Correspondence falters, scarcely has it begun. A kind of epistolary curse has spread over the planet, blocking off the natural human instinct to respond to a question, exhortation or other stimulus. Of course decent people do not simply throw letters away, but put them in files marked 'Unanswered Correspondence', which enables them to maintain a certain overview and thus after receiving a letter from A reply to a letter from N, whose letter has now lain a sufficient time in the file. Some even acquire a certain virtuosity in the filing of correspondence: I still admire to this day one notable academic administrator, who separated his letters specially into primary letters, reminders, or secondary letters, and reminders of reminders, i.e. tertiary letters, and only ever dealt with the latter, and that only when the pile ceased to hold together and threatened to collapse. This was systematic handling of correspondence on the gravity principle, and one can only respect greatly a human mode of behaviour so intimately at one with natural forces.

The declining appetite for letter writing is balanced of course by a still strong and robust instinctive desire to receive letters, or rather the ideal kind of letter, announcing to us the favour of the angelic choirs, selection for a representative team, invitation to a country house, a large annuity or tax relief, a gift from Brazil, appointment as an esteemed corresponding member, a letter moreover requiring no answer, beyond a picture-postcard of Prague: the Charles Bridge. This instinct is sorely threatened however by the slump in correspondence.

Fortunately there is one other, evidently metaphysical principle in operation, which prevents the complete collapse of epistolary communication. It is the principle of crossed letters. When we are very eager for an answer to a letter of ours, we eventually resolve to write a second. The writing, not to mention sending, postal sorting and dispatching of this second letter, evokes in some people – presumably more sensitive to correspondence – a reply to the first letter; this normally arrives the day after you send off the reminder. The principle of crossed letters leads to a state where neither party any longer knows what has already been replied to and what has not, but it is nevertheless the only hope we have. Without this principle we would probably never receive a response. It almost always turns out that the reply they owed you was written at the same time as your reminder, and thus was inspired by some kind of telepathic synchronisation of the two correspondents. If we are not believers in telepathy, which we are not, we are forced to propose some kind of ripening mechanism in the internalised time frames of the two correspondents, but this is a mere theoretical detail. In practice it is a fact that the writing of a letter elicits a reply to the previous letter, and this is a powerful and relatively reliable general law.

Only extremely hardened and refractory souls are never affected by it. To those it is probably better never to write at all.

You will, I am sure, agree with me that if page 534 finds us only in the second chapter, the length of the first one must have been really intolerable.
ARTHUR CONAN DOYLE, 1859-1930,
in the words of Sherlock Holmes

On Reading

Francis Bacon wrote: Reading maketh a full man; conference a ready man; and writing an exact man. Francis Bacon lived a long time ago, and this makes the second and third part of his observation hard for us to comprehend today. It may however still be possible to reflect on the initial part. What reading do we here have in mind? The Epic of Gilgamesh as well as *User Instructions for Infra-Red Bathroom Radiator Type 512*? Claude Bernard's *Introduction à l'étude de la médecine expérimentale* as well as ads in the Personal Column? The strict person of learning would certainly reject such lumping together as inadmissible, for Gilgamesh's encounter with the wild man Enkidu is held to constitute a crucial cultural landmark, whereas the information that the minimum safe distance according to Czechoslovak norm 73 07 69 for the placing of inflammable substances in front of an infra-red radiator is 0.6 of a metre is a trivial matter immaterial to human self-fulfilment. I cannot help thinking however that the person whose kitchen-bathroom area has gone up in flames is much more humanly deprived than he who is uninformed on the Great Flood and the Babylonian 'Noah' Utnapishtim. I even reckon the insight a piece of writing on vivisection may give into the anxieties, tribulations, joys and sorrows of an age is not totally unlike the effect of reading that some woman, dark hair, 26, 168cm, own flat, two children, seeks friend under 30 for forest rambles. I myself, I admit, read with undying interest chess reports accompanied by Grand Masters' temperamental commentaries, in spite of not having the faintest idea what is going on, and on public transport I study the Regulations for Conveyance of Passengers with care, even though I am not conveying on my person any readily combustible materials, nor any animals in any form of container, and even though I do think they ought to be written in logical clear language. I just want to be a full man.

On these grounds I suggest that it is not only content and literary form that is fundamental to reading, but the act of reading itself. That is to say, the act of absorption. Of being transported somewhere slightly different. A small step out of the action going on around into an action imaginably going on somewhere else, out

of one's own story, which we constantly try to make sense of, into a story which we need not try to make sense of, whether it be the monster Huwawa, the ticket inspector, bathroom unit B3, or the Indian Defence and the existence of a healthy out-of-doors dark-haired lady.

I know not what Bacon meant by fullness, but he certainly said reading, not literature. Instructions are not literature, and literature is not instruction, even if people sometimes mix the two. But reading is reading, the decipherment of letter codes, and this presupposes a certain engrossment. And so by fullness let us now mean something like alternation, alteration and succession of deed and thought, not excluding even the humble infra-red radiator.

**Try to learn something about everything
and everything about something.**
Text on the memorial of
THOMAS HENRY HUXLEY, 1895

Sand-Glasses

The English poet Samuel Taylor Coleridge, born over two hundred years ago, once wrote: 'Readers may be divided into four classes: 1. Sponges, who absorb all they read, and return it nearly in the same state, only a little dirtied. 2. Sand-glasses, who retain nothing, and are content to get through a book for the sake of getting through the time. 3. Strain-bags, who retain merely the dregs of what they read, and return it nearly in the same state, only a little dirtied. 4. Mogul diamonds, equally rare and valuable, who profit by what they read, and [reflecting, refracting and enlarging upon it] enable others to profit by it also.'

These then are possibly the kinds of readers to be found up to the present day, and I reckon it would be interesting to know if any group or class is expanding or contracting, as time flies by, conditions change and with them the significance of reading, and as literature becomes further differentiated.

Another problem is what class of readers a given author or editor presupposes.

A special case in point is popular science. Even though you might think that we read works of popular science in order to learn something in a popular fashion, and even though this writing is all about scientific activity, which is, says G.A. Sarton, 'the only one which is obviously and undoubtedly cumulative and progressive', many practitioners of this writing seem mostly to believe that it is read only by the afore-mentioned sand-glasses. Sand-glasses, which retain nothing, but at the point of reading notoriously forget even the last remnants of their school education, so that everything has to be given to them on a plate, you have to begin from square one, from Adam and Eve, explaining of course in simple straightforward words who Adam was, and that evidently he never existed at all, being only a fiction of Scripture, while his partner was the non-existent Eve, along with the serpent, a vertebrate of the class Reptilia, renowned for having no legs, in the case of the slow-worm mere hidden rudimentary ones.

Many writers of popular science thus either doubt mostly the efficacy of what was written in the past, or judge that a decisive majority of their readers – insofar as they are not mere sand-glasses – are a totally helpless crowd of youngsters, possessing neither dictionary nor encyclopaedia, and experiencing their first real encounter with a book. Sometimes I get the impression that they are judging from their own introspection.

Which brings us to the point, that popular science is basically non-cumulative (= non-increasing) in nature, leaving aside any question of its putative progressive (= improving) character.

Theoreticians – use vanishing ink!

KAREL KONRAD

1960

Books That Go to Oblivion

We regard the books which fill our library bookshelves as somehow immortal. I know of nobody who without some reason akin to moving house, redecorating or fire would take down his books and classify them into books for the rubbish and books for further sojourn on the shelves. Books once acquired become a kind of permanent accustomed part of our micro-environment, of our spiritual integument, a kind of bodily covering, and who would ever rip the feathers from his body, when a bird would never do any such thing. In cases of dire necessity volumes surplus to requirements and alien to spiritual needs are carried off to second-hand bookshops, whereby they are enabled to continue their literary existence. Even our own modest libraries contain the endeavours of several generations, and the holdings of venerable and mighty mega-libraries are a kind of general treasure-house of the nation, a kind of material memory, which endures, albeit largely unused. Indeed, culture in general endures, albeit largely unused.

Then I was surprised by the news (F. Greve, *Philadelphia Inquirer*), that books manufactured in the United States since about 1840 in fact auto-destruct. Up to that time the paper was made of rags and dipped in gelatine, so that the ink would not run. From that time on they began for reasons of economy to print on paper made of wood and dipped in substances which react with atmospheric moisture and give rise to sulphuric acid. The decomposing cellulose likewise gives rise to acidic by-products, and the book disintegrates. This applies to books printed up to the beginning of this century. Valuable works can of course be preserved on microfilm, but a huge amount of documents, popular reading matter and bound volumes of journals will disappear all by themselves from the shelves by the end of the twentieth century. It is not thus the case that everything that has ever been printed and that survives outward calamity endures at least in some depository or other. It endureth not, it passeth away, out of mind, but also out of this world. I do not know why this bothers one, but it does. Maybe it is because even those books which flit from human memory are automatically and without reference to their age considered of potential existential value. Probably it is the case that we wish to have somewhere at our disposal that which we have failed to read and register in living memory over the last hundred years, hoping that we or our successors will acquire in time the extra brain potential, and that the old flour will yet be turned into bread. It will not. Not even this system of immortality is whole and perfect. There will survive only the skeletal remains of the catalogues and classification numbers. Insofar as they were entered on adequate paper. What we have not read now, may never be read by anyone.

I have been reading much more carefully of late, trying to detect any possible sourness in the savour.

> **Only that which brings something quite new is really worthy of the name of a book.**
> CHRISTOPH LICHTENBURG
> 1742-99

The Mythology of Books

It is hard to say why we are so attached to books. After all, for information storage and retrieval we have microfilms and computer memories, which save a huge amount of space and time. For visual beauty we have slides, film strips, and video, which can communicate a thing to us from a projector much more faithfully, authentically, and radiantly than any printed book, however good.

It is hard to say why we crave, sitting or lying, to strain our eyes with those stacks of ridiculously tiny letters, somewhat ill-adapted to our vision, breaking the binding of the book at the spine, preventing breezes accidentally turning the pages, marking important passages with pieces of paper or something. After all we could always have great literature on tape and listen to it in the finest performances; specialist data, if no computer is available, are handled in any case mainly in the form of notes, cards in files, and xerox copies of fragments of fragments.

It is hard to say why we regard our books as such an integral part of our intellectual existence, why we pack them up and haul them off with us when we move house, like a clod of native soil, and why we feel not altogether at home again until that personal, partly read and partly unread library is once more unpacked and placed at the mercy of dust, the museum (or carpet) beetle and mouldering rot.

I suppose it is like this: the book is a myth, the book is a cultural myth of coherence and affinity with personal history and the history of the species. For the writer and reader, and even the mere looker, a book means more than it is. It is an intimate record, a private record of the public domain, a familiar old record of both the old new and the new new, it is newness reified, which remains itself. And yet is intimate. A book is a close intimation of the world.

In a certain sense however also a world in itself. It provides a clothbound or paperbacked world with a beginning and an end, a graspable world, accessible to the habitual paths of the senses and the mind, palpable and secure in the face of the infinite, the unending, unbound and unquiet world of multiplicity, chance, entropy and decay. Something like a small soft sphere containing the larger rough sphere of the world; a bounded discourse containing and therefore encapsulating all unboundedness.

In this sense the book is a cult object, ennobled both by the ages and – let us hope – by the best available techniques of spirit and hand. The form of a book, the visual worth of a book is and will be more and more important, the more books in their function of information compendia are replaced by other means, other technologies. And maybe one will return yet to the sense and value of the old illuminated chronicles, now that the zenith days of book learning and specialised library-acquired erudition seem to have passed.

Science is for those who learn; poetry for those who know.
JOSEPH ROUX
1834-86

Poetry in the Year 2000

I was gratified to learn from M. Malita's *Chronicle of the Year 2000* (dated 1973) that the author believes poetry will still survive in ages to come. Though I know of no one who thinks otherwise (poetry not being some penguin that might one day become extinct), nevertheless every effort to weave this magical occupation into our picture of the future is praiseworthy, as this picture all too often seems to consist of nothing but wires, computer experts and concrete caves. Poetry is not a literary concoction, but a live experience, a mode of sensing and relating to one's surroundings. If someone, anyone is bewitched by a thing, animated, moved or activated, he becomes – at least for himself – a creator of poetry. And now and then someone writes it down and someone publishes it.

I believe moreover that the subjects of poetry are not simply country lanes, old cottages and young butterflies. I even take the view that the sources of poetry today and tomorrow, poetry as a mode of experiencing and a mode of writing, are more the motorway than the mire, more the city lights than farmyard manure, and more the swish of the transmission wheel than the rustle of graveyard blooms, even though one has a much greater tradition than the other.

Poetry as literature even has certain felicities and advantages over and above other forms of art: as Malita himself says, above all in its conciseness, density and immediacy. Poetry happens in the minimum of space and the minimum of time, and that in it-self makes it modern and gives it a future. In addition, in its close links with the vis-ual arts, music and drama, it has for some time been anticipating new forms of total, synthetic art. And lastly, having long been more than conveyance of information, having been a close immediate bond between people and people and things, it will not suffer the crisis of other forms, the crisis of the less than totally well-informed author in a world brimful with scientific and other weird pieces of information, the crisis of the less than totally erudite author in a world inhabited by erudite and more or less even wise experts. I do not mean by this that poetry will be the preserve of God's simpletons; it will also be a place where the developed intellect can reveal not only its ingenuity, but also its simplicity. Not only its retrospective nostalgias, but also its pathways to new domiciles.

So I am not worried about poetry in the year 2000. If anything I am worried about the poets.

Choice of Limits

The more constraints one imposes, the more one frees
one's self of the chains that shackle the spirit...
the arbitrariness of the constraint only serves
to obtain precision of execution.

IGOR STRAVINSKY
1882-1971

Caution is the stepmother of wisdom.
KAREL KONRÁD
1960

The Differentiating Instinct

The differentiating instinct is inseparably linked with the imitative one, or is even identical with it. It is its inner reflection and image. For we only imitate anyone and anything with the intention of being different, of developing our own "I" along our own lines, different from all other "I's" encountered along the way. Discovering for example that all around us a certain style of hair or beard is increasing in frequency, we soon realise that the originality of our soul and the handsomeness of our figure demand immediate emphasis by adopting the same cut and the same shape of beard. We are insistent that our own hair (and beard) will be somehow inwardly different, above all because it is ours. The same applies of course to bodices and shades of eyelids, and so we have fashion sections and fashion salons. Fashion in this sense is the attempt to be the same on the surface and yet to feel different within.

In our childhood our differentiating instinct makes us skip over unbeaten, even flatly unrecommended tracks. In our adulthood – something which these days we somehow reach in this respect rather early – the differentiating instinct sort of curls up deep down inside us, away from the sphere of action into the sphere of self-explanation, self-persuasion and self-directed rhetoric. We say We Would Set About It Quite Differently (if we wanted to), When We Tackle Something Like This (but mostly we don't), We Have A Mind Of Our Own (but mostly this mind is replaced in actual fact by the pocket and other organs). Originality and irreplaceable deeds are turned into a conditional complex sentence. The distinctive instinct, which used to be the true brother of courage and self-sacrifice, degenerates into the garrulous uncle of sloth and conformity.

This transformation has nothing to do with collectivism, or with the essence of life under pressure. Every project, every common act requires individual courage, non-duplicated and non-conformist diligence, originality not in costume but in the so-called heart of the matter.

It is only through originality in heart and mind, something naturally hard to instil, that the distinctive instinct could somehow once and for all divorce itself from the imitative instinct, and become a creative formative principle in the life of individuals and society as a whole. But still, when it comes to actual deeds there is really no time left for instincts anyway.

A gadget has been made for the selective removal of weeds,
a container for dirty nappies that plays a lullaby,
a plastic board that can hold the cards for players
confined to their beds,
a cooling ventilator for the windows of small aeroplanes,
a car safety-belt for cats and dogs,
a gadget for solo free-style wrestling,
an invisible goldfish,
a child's swing driven by a petrol engine,
a transistorised golf-ball with an electronic tracker,
a WC that flushes upwards from below,
an automatic drinks cabinet server,
as well as a storage system of ideas containing up to 13,000 words
on plastic cards.

A. SLANGE
1975

Garden Gnomes

Those plaster gnomes, staring vacantly in our gardens, used always to be the epitome of the degenerate taste of the gardener responsible. I wish to declare that for present day purposes I regard the garden gnome as a pleasant life-enhancing thing: it is basically merry, even when it is sad; not even the gardener responsible takes it entirely seriously. That which we do not take entirely seriously, is at least a bit of fun, and fun is enlivening, and what is enlivening is not evil, in spite of any conflict there might be with aesthetic standards. After all, every second, indeed every first flower-bed (not to mention rockery!) is partly in conflict with the aesthetic norms of garden architecture, and try telling anyone that.

In that sense the real garden gnomes are not garden gnomes. On the contrary garden gnomes are the crystal chandeliers, wrought-iron grilles, porcelain figurines and Egyptian reliefs that we stuff our interiors with en masse – with the mighty aid of manufacturers and buyers – in order to give them the air of a Baroque sanctuary,

Rococo hareem or hut of some Egyptian fellah who snitched a few excavated finds from the pyramids.

These sorts of garden gnomes spread like influenza to the accompaniment of tape-recorded background music, elaborately tiled fireplaces, and plastic everywhere, they spread with such mortal solemnity that any discussion of them is seen as sacrilege and rejection of the good life.

I would lay bets that the first setter-in-motion of these gnomish brigades was an impulse from abroad, where, thirty years or so ago, there was a mass burgeoning of art and antiques shops selling more or less exactly what our attics are stuffed with. The other was undoubtedly the cultivation of cottage life, which asks that one keep a wagon wheel in the garden and inside the house a coffee mill and an oil lamp adorned with a picture of storks in flight. Both these phenomena were unfortunately received with neo-romantic passion and the only funny side consisted of the isolated efforts of a few modern interior designers.

And since the aesthetic standards of experts have virtually no influence on anyone, I suppose that these gnomes must be treated as a totally extra-aesthetic phenomenon, expressions of an existential game, playing at something, a game in which we are all ultimately involved at least in a minor way, a game in which there is no comparison to what should or could be, just as there is no comparison between a game of cards and chess.

And the only expression of taste I would request is that in this game, as in any other, we should not take ourselves much too seriously. There are quite simply these things called gnomes, and there is nothing more embarrassing than gnomes trying to make themselves out to be Pallas Athene.

Emotion, the mother of all authenticity.
And kitschiness was corrupted – by art.
KAREL KONRÁD
1960

Kitsch

According to dictionary definitions kitsch is literary, musical, visual or theatrical creation masquerading as art, but in fact aiming merely at cheap appeal. An exhibition of kitsch art at Roztoky Castle near Prague, the high point of which was in my view the modern mass-produced furniture, aroused to judge from the visitors' book a frenetically positive response. You see, the public is divided into one small section which goes to exhibitions, condemns cheap appeal and debased taste, and another much larger section that happily consumes and makes the stuff and does not go to exhibitions. In the visitors' book I enjoyed most of all the entry of one schoolboy, who expressed his burning desire to possess a garden gnome just like the one on show. This schoolboy, who presumably had not read my article on the same subject, here confirmed my impression that the garden gnome is today more or less innocent fun and games, and that the true aesthetic vermin are polished walnut chiffoniers garnished with empty bottles of Cognac.

But the schoolboy aspiring to possess a plaster gnome indicates a more serious problem: 1. He was exposed to children's picture books, which are based on the fantasy principle of realistic depiction of fairies and forest bogles; a fairy in the shape of a decently dressed and nicely made-up young miss is realistic and admissible, a fairy in the form of a stroke, blotch or blur probably upsets the child's approach to objective reality. 2. However this may be, a gnome with a beard, shorts and a little rake makes him happy, and a simple pebble, which used to delight him as a toddler, now leaves him cold, for his environment teaches him that the beautiful is not pure and simple, but only artful, full-colour-illustrated and "meaning something".

Why then is the schoolboy not to be given the garden gnome that would bring him such joy? Because it would be cheap joy? Because it would be joy out of foolishness, not out of art? But is there not perhaps only one form of joy, not graded according to its acquisition value and the psychological or sociological mechanism that induces it? Perhaps it is a fact, that once we have deprived a child of joy out of simple pebbles, it is hard for us to deny him more questionable sources of aesthetic pleasure. On the other hand where is the harm in this "cheapness"? In this cheap appeal? I think it lies in the the way it blocks the path to gradually acquiring a sense of the beautiful and hence one's general bearings in the world. Moreover, the pleasure the boy takes in the gnome is a source of dreams and playful imaginings; but the pleasure the worthy citizen takes in the chiffonier with its Cognac bottles and artificial flowers is an empty and conservative proprietorial pleasure, which creates nothing more than that and recognises nothing more than that. And from sluggish distinctions between the beautiful and the appealing it is only a short step to sluggish criteria of good and honest and bad and evil.

I believe therefore that the problem of kitsch is not merely one of aesthetics, but also one of morality.

> **There are performances**
> **where the public is quite without talent.**
> LOUIS JOUVET
> 1887-1951

On Reflex Haste

We went to a cinema performance. The film was extremely interesting and moreover it was one of those experimental-era films where the credits come up at the end. For those two reasons we stayed sitting in our seats. Unfortunately, three minutes before the end it was clear that the end was nigh, for the music started playing very loud and the heroes went off mid-screen towards a blackened horizon (it was an unhappy ending, otherwise they would have gone off into the sun). As soon as the music began to play very loud, three-quarters of the audience got up and fled, trampling the weak and sick underfoot. As soon as the heroes began to make for the horizon, the rest of the public stampeded out in a panic. The usherette came over and bade us go home, as they were locking up. We pointed out that the film was still running and said we wanted to stay to the end. The good lady remarked that anybody could see the film was over, she wanted to get home too, and would we kindly get out immediately. Then the credits went up and two minutes later both picture and sound ceased. We crawled out in the dark through some kind of side door and were assailed by the staff with expressions of gross annoyance and vice versa.

That is what happens to those who fail to hurry at the right time and place: that is to say, when "everybody else" is hurrying, seized by an unconditional reflex urge to be somewhere else, having been in the same place two hours in a row. It is evidently risky to submit to cultural regulations when some reflex regulation is triggered off and commands a mass stampede.

Similarly risky behaviour is exhibited by those who submit to traffic regulations and wait at pedestrian crossings until the green man lights up. Here the ordinary citizen submits of course only to subcortical mechanisms and endeavours to cross on the red, in order to perform merry scenes of leapings among oncoming vehicles, deliver abuse to horrified drivers and proudly gain the opposite pavement, stopping thereupon for a little chat and commenting on those poor miserable specimens still on the other side and wasting fifteen seconds of their natural lives.

It is naive of me of course, but I think that a civilised and cultivated person (whatever that is supposed to be) should hurry only when impelled by need, not by reflex. The reflex urge to be somewhere else, unconditionally and at once, is a sign of senile dementia on the one hand and mass neurosis on the other. It leads to a state of affairs in which we are never ever not in a hurry, in which we are never where we ought to be, and in which the right time in life is permanently somewhere else, for example on the other side of the highway.

We never amplify our passage through life by reflex haste, we only make it more chaotic, even if obeying reflexes feels at times extremely pleasant to some. If you feel the same, then finish reading this quickly, hurl the printed page aside, belt across the street a few times, cut in front of five people in the next queue, leave work at least five minutes early, take all the short cuts across the grass in the park, and depart to your place of final rest: no doubt you will get there ahead of the others, ready to take your well-earned repose from reflex haste. Unless that is you return to haunt us.

Order is Heaven's first law.
ALEXANDER POPE
1688-1744

The Intrusion of Pallas Athene

It happened in Warsaw, but let's admit it could just as easily have been in Prague. It was one of those festivals at which various wisdoms are lectured upon; one of the sessions took place in some sort of district library, at an evening hour. Those who were to lecture arrived at the venue, and those who were to listen likewise, and the lecturing began after the usual obligatory delay. The lecturing went ahead nicely, those who were meant to keep their mouths shut kept their mouths shut, and those who were meant to lecture lectured. However, after fifteen minutes the door suddenly opened behind the lecturer's back and a stalwart woman of a certain indefinite age stood in the doorway, wielding a bucket and a cloth on a broomstick. In the spiritualised atmosphere of the room she reminded one faintly of Pallas Athene, without the owl of course. For a moment she questioningly scrutinised the ambient spirituality, then swept it aside as it were and marched with stalwart step to the back of the hall. There she commenced not without noise to clear away the unoccupied chairs and mop the floor in the vacated areas. After a while one of the organisers hurrying over began in a powerful stage whisper persuading Athene of the untimely nature of this activity. But the good woman remonstrated with him firmly, followed now by the serious majority of the audience, who found this realistic cameo scene somehow rather appealing. The good woman, conscious of her rights, did not lower herself to a whisper, but maintained that, as the hour of six o'clock had struck, she was to clean the hall, no changes to her duties having been stated. Consequently the hall would be cleaned, and then proceedings could continue. Order must be observed. And insofar as proceedings were to continue, a spare key would have to be used, because she was going to lock up at seven o'clock as per instructions. And so it was to be. The lecturing was more or less disturbed, lecturers and listeners driven by energetic sweeps of the broom into remote parts of the hall, the hall was swept, chairs placed on top of chairs, and the table wiped by way of conclusion. Athene gazed thereupon triumphantly over her works with the look of a creator, battler against entropy and saviour of order, then grasped the bucket and tucked the broom neatly under one arm and locked the hall from the outside. Whereupon the lecturing and listening continued, an act of some hardihood, for it was unclear whether the spare key existed, or whether one would have to climb out the window.

Later on some of us claimed this was due to lack of organisation. Others among us said however that on the contrary it was a victory for order. The first said it was not a matter of whether the cleaning was done, but of whether wisdom was propagated. The others said however that the propagation of wisdom was arguably nothing other itself than the propagation of order, and therefore took no priority over any other propagation of order. On the contrary, there had occurred a praiseworthy – though unplanned – blending of the two kinds of order, and surely two kinds of order are better than one. And, we said, would that the propagators of wisdom were as persistent as the said Pallas Athene.

**It is not true that women break secrets,
the truth is, they pass them on unbroken,
retaining the bloom and beauty of their mystery.**
KAREL ČAPEK
1926

On the Classification of Mystery

Depths and distances are mysterious, perhaps everyone will recognise that. Depths of night, depths of time, depths of the universe, depths of a lake, depths of distant or ancient towns, depths of the inscrutable future. In old castles, where mystery is included in the entrance fee, the most notoriously mysterious, and hence attractive, sights are deep dungeons and deep wells. Gloom or darkness reigns there, you aren't allowed to go down there and you can't see inside. Mystery arises where you can't go and your senses can't reach. Your senses and your rational sense.

They cannot reach and as a rule do not wish to. For the mysterious has a recreational function and there is no need to reach into the depths if it is not part of our stipulated contractual duties.

Maybe for this reason we safely create for ourselves our own handy little mysteries; our own little everyday depths. I for example cannot shake off the impression that those whom I visit have some other room in their homes which I never see, some door through which I never pass. That in their privacy however slender they are engaged in some activity unknown to me, but vital. That in their time there exists some hidden backwater, just as there exists a tapering space in the cellar under the spiral stairs, a space which never was and never will be either a well or a dungeon, but is all the more mysterious for being neither.

In some vague way I trust and believe in these mysteries and do not try to penetrate them. I do not envy those who try. I find indeed that I need these mysteries for my peace of mind: if I train my colleague to carry out some procedure, let us say to mix something, heat it and let it set, during the act itself I go away or look the other way. I believe, you see, that he himself puts something inscrutable, yet vital, into the simplest little sequence of operations, and that the mixing and setting will happen much better if I am not able to watch. The mysterious unknown and non-existent act gives me greater peace of mind and optimism that it will set perfectly. Mostly it doesn't.

Indubitably I may be suspected of magic thinking, a fond relic of childhood. But I know for certain that others behave similarly, and as regards their own body (not to mention so-called soul) practically everybody does: even the most high-powered biologists and physicians regard their own livers not merely as a series of enzyme processes and waves of cellular alarms, struggles and deaths, but as a powerful mysterious organ, capable of withstanding any amount of attack from alcohol and other nasty substances. They regard their own lungs not as a readily combustible wisp of tissue equipped with a positively crisis-ridden epithelium, but as the pathologically exempt bellows of an inward dancing bagpiper. Those who are deceived in this private mysteriously ebulliant optimism frequently resort to creating the opposite depth of scepticism and fear, sensing the woodworm at work in every drawer of their organism. In each case these organic mysteries relieve one to a certain extent of the duty to take care: even the nearest and smallest of mysteries is beyond reach.

The mysteries in our lives which we actually try to tackle are those of medium distance and medium extent.

The Greatest Power of Man

The greatest power available to man is not to use it

MEISTER ECKHART

ca 1260-1327

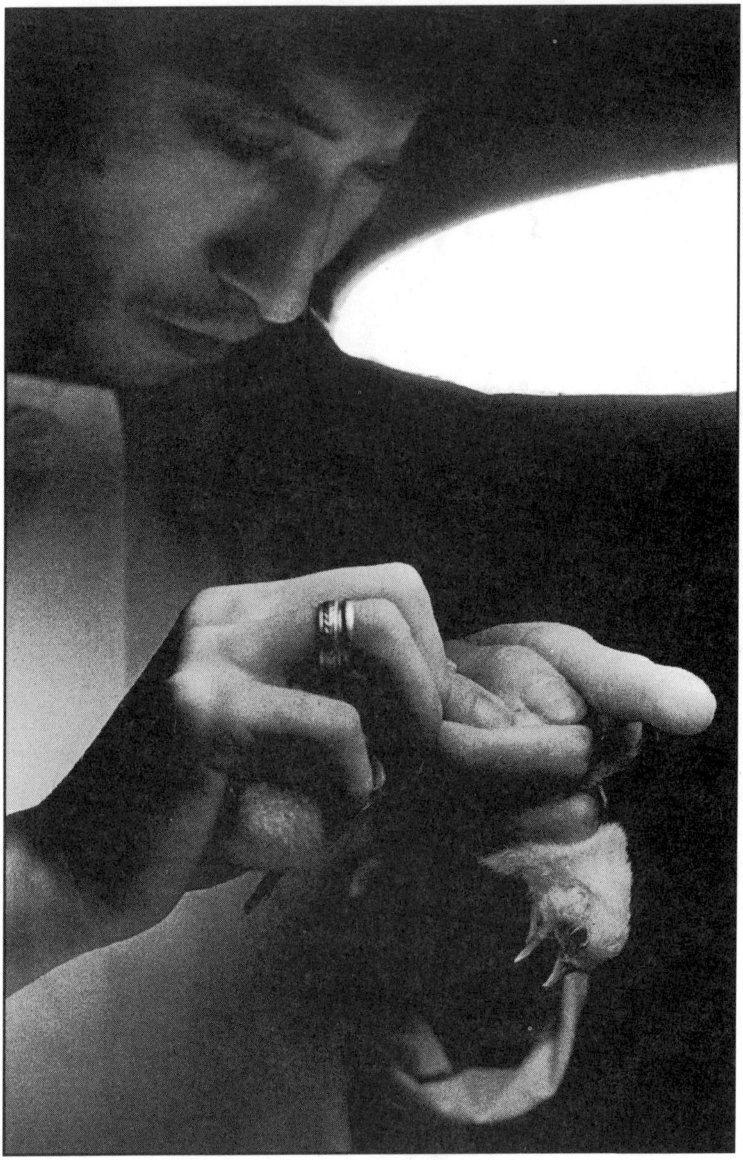

> **Many ancient, ancestral mechanisms persisting in modern man have to find some outlet, even if they no longer correspond to any real needs.**
> RENÉ DUBOS
> 1965

Towards the Physiology of Joy

Christmas as a season of joy poses us a number of basic questions. Christmas is clearly a cause for joy, whereas joy is not a cause for Christmas, otherwise we would never get away from it. If Christmas is a cause for joy, it must also be stated that there are known to be simpler and organisationally less demanding causes for joy than it. Joy may be caused in us merely by meeting a decent person who is still alive, by the scoring of a goal, the finding of a four-leaved clover, handkerchief or mislaid diary, likewise by the sight of a clear sky. It is nevertheless the custom, that we do not all look at once – experiencing lovely joyful sensations – up at the sky, but all at once organise our Christmas tide, even if it does all at once cause no small difficulties with transport, shopping and the maintenance of uninterrupted services.

It is of course the case, that however much joy, even so-called pure joy is the aim intended, there is in fact nothing of the sort. There is no joy as such. There is only joy at finding one's diary, joy at scoring a goal, heaven-gazing joy, joy at meeting a decent person who is still alive, and joy at Christmas. If joys were interchangeable, it would indeed be possible to choose the simplest and technically most advanced: let us say joy produced by stimulating certain cerebral zones...Even in man stimulating certain cerebral zones can produce positive emotional states which may be described as "joy" or "relaxation", whereas stimulating others produces unpleasant feelings which may be described as "tension", "fear", "anger", "anxiety", "restlessness". There seems to be a bigger choice of unpleasant ones. The problem is however that different patients feel different states when identical, or probably identical cerebral zones are stimulated. And the same person may have very different feelings when the same zone is stimulated at different times. It is simply not true that stimulating the brain in a certain way can produce repeatedly the same emotional state, the same memories and the same behaviour. The brain, as E.S. Valenstein says (in *Psychology*

Today 12, 1978), is not organised into clear sections corresponding to the categories which we use to classify individual states and behaviour...Neither "joy" nor "aggression" nor even "anxiety" is a function of a distinct unit of the nervous system, but it is an abstract psychological concept. It is certainly possible to induce relatively uniform and episodically pleasant feelings using various forms of poison and mild intoxication, this however is about as much like pure joy as passing through a canal is like sailing a boat on the open seas.

And so we must settle for joy as it is, the joys of Christmas too, allowing that they differ from year to year, like memories, and like hopes.

Like diaries also, and decent people.

The brain is the means
by which we think
we think.
JULIAN TUWIM
1894-1953

Dwelling in Thought

One day a famous physiologist of ours, one more adept in laboratory work than most, was visited by a friend of the microbiological persuasion. When the door opened, this busy laboratory-adept physiologist turned out not to be holding any instrument in his hand, or any book physiological or otherwise, he was just sitting staring blue-eyed out of the window. When asked what he was doing he responded: Oh, just sitting and thinking, Zdeněk, but mostly just sitting...

I reckon that this sentence caught the gist unusually well of that odd state of dwelling in thought, a state strikingly unlike any real thinking, not to mention effortful thinking. In a state of real thinking, which is, as we know, far from painless, ideas and syntactic fragments race through the head and are marshalled with many an inward jolt into more or less provisional trains of thought, intended to get one somewhere and put over something of substance on the way. Put over, put across, convey. Thinking therefore is not unlike railwaymen's shunting in a marshalling yard. And as a rule the tracks are fairly overburdened and there is a dearth of space, and not enough stop blocks, known as chocks or scotches.

Dwelling in thought however is more akin to a stopping train, in which at first you wait and wait, then you go along for a bit and wait again, all in idyllic surroundings with nice tiny little stations, where the clucking of hens mingles harmoniously with the bell signals from afar and the intermittent whistle of the guard. On such a journey nothing is urgently sought after, nothing is feverishly expected, and reaching one's destination is taken more as a bonus reward for submissive patience. Dwelling in thought is an occupation devoid of pressures and pulls, an occupation in which not all that much happens, but equally little is lost; discoveries made are few, but pure and untrammelled, somehow already familiar, like pearls of the deep, to be brought to the surface and dried, discoveries marked by the words – Ah, so that's how it is, just as I thought. However little the thinker, or rather here ponderer, actually thought, when really it just flashed distantly and vaguely through the mind, or else he read it somewhere or other, just in passing, no need to find the quotation. Nor would he be able to.

If we read therefore in Loren Eiseley's last book that (even the great) Darwin took his main ideas of natural selection from the work of Edward Blythe, whom he fails to cite in this connection, we ascribe it to Darwin's having sometime after 1835 (when Blythe's communication appeared) just been sitting and thinking, but mostly just sitting, and suddenly Blythe's premises and his own reflections from the deck of the *Beagle* purely and simply united in the shape of so-it's-like-that-just-as-I-thought...

Which does not mean, when you open the door and the occupant of the room is staring blue-eyed out of the window, that a new *Origin of the Species* is en route. It only may be, so long as the starer is a Darwin. In any event it is best to open other people's doors with polite discretion.

> **Tradition is a most momentous,**
> **practically maternal cycle;**
> **not merely the charm of deficiency.**
> KAREL KONRÁD
> 1960

A Professor on a Bike

If there is anything about man that can be adequately described by the laws of mechanics, it is the motion produced by muscles and joints. Indeed it has already been expressed by a series of equations fed into a computer in distant Madison, USA. In the course of a decade it has proved feasible to account for all kinds of movements of the human body from walking to chewing.

All this had an extremely practical aim in mind, the computer is now able, given specific weights and measures, to plot an optimal rehabilitation plan for a damaged joint, calculate a prognosis or select the best possible mode of surgical orthopaedic intervention. Which it does.

The computer would even be able to model a mobile robot, which by means of wires, rods and motors could carry out any human locomotive function, with the least imaginable wastage of energy.

It turned out of course that man does not in fact operate on the principle of a machine working with minimum wastage of energy. When the computer model was used to analyse the movements of a top gymnast, it was found that the subject moved with practically maximum inefficiency and lack of economy. Researcher A. Seireg accounts for this by suggesting that both consciously and unconsciously we conform above all not to laws of economy, but to laws of beauty. The gymnast's movements were as uneconomical as they were beautiful. Or elegant, something of course which is beyond the machine's grasp.

Somewhere involved in this I suspect is a further consideration, which I would term endemic idiosyncrasy. I am led to this view by the example of one local classical philologist, who – perhaps as a form of protest against the world of the motor-car – moves about exclusively by bicycle. He does this in spite of the fact that the year before last he fell and gave himself a fracture of the skull base. He does this in fact to the detriment of classical philology. Graced with a beard and overcoat flapping over the bicycle chain he passes and nods at passers-by. Nodding, he loses his balance and falls. Nimbly he mounts again and rides off to encounter further passers-by. The passers-by try to hide on glimpsing him in the distance, in order not to occasion further mishaps, but all in vain. Always there is someone to whom to nod. Even for a picnic in secluded meadows and a walk in the forest the venerable professor arrives by bicycle, lagging only a little behind, mounting and falling in the wake of those on foot.

According to both the principles of mechanics and the principles of aesthetics his mode of motion is dysfunctional, indeed futile. Nonetheless, bicycle motion is the motion of his choice and he holds to it, as if it were a classical tradition from the time of the Trojan Wars. His motion across the globe has a certain effect of pathos, making one reflect upon whether the bicycle was not perhaps the invention after all of Ulysses.

In any event the said classical philologist is a serious warning in the face of the hope that the whole of man might one day be modelled on the computer. Our daily rounds and routines will doubtless be carried out by supremely efficient economic robots. But amongst them always some classical philologist will be found and nodding as he goes. Which is not despair, but hope in hope.

Some problems are just too complicated
for rational logical solutions.
They admit of insights, not answers.
JEROME BERT WIESNER
1963

On Gazing

Use of the optical analytic organ is denoted by a whole number of words with delicate shades of meaning, which may be placed in order of ascending intensity of action: glance, look, stare; gaze, gape, gawp. Etc. Individual verbs furthermore may be decorated with various appendages, whose poetic vigour serves to distinguish other delicate nuances: thus we can say (in Czech) you stare like a goose peering into a bottle, or as if your toys had fallen down a drain, a person gapes like a bug at a chemist's shop, or gawps like a mouse turned up by the plough. These subtle distinctions were inspired by life itself and I reckon we cannot do without them, as when for example we want to write a travel piece on how life is lived in other parts. In some places people mainly just take a look, in others they quite unambiguously stare. For example in New York nobody takes a first look (at other people, I mean), whereas in El Paso they take a look and move a couple of miles on down the road, and in Ciudad Juarez, they gawp.

How is it with us? There are regional differences, no doubt, but in general I would say, that here one gazes. For instance I had to get out of a parking spot where the car was tightly jammed up between another two vehicles. A man passing by, seeing me twist the steering wheel, stopped and began to gaze. If he had just glanced, or looked, it might probably have occurred to him to indicate how much gap I had in front and behind, such people do exist. If he had gawped, he would probably have riled me, and I would have requested this little service myself. However, he merely gazed. Gazing is an only mildly offensive, slightly impertinent activity; gazing is more a matter of self-absorption, dimly sizing up the object of observation, an activity on the borderline between merely registering and actually contemplating. It is an evidently pleasant activity, in which we avoid the strain of either concentration or ratiocination. An activity which is an end in itself and elicits no further activity. So this good man gazed away, while I inched forward left a little, and back right a little. When I drove away, the man was still there gazing, showing not a sign of mental life, as it follows from the essence of gazing.

It was then that I resolved to conduct an experiment. I stopped, switched off the engine, and began gazing at him from inside the car. I took great care not to deviate either in the direction of the goose and the bottle, or in the direction of the bug and the chemist's shop, which would have amounted to a form of assault on the good man. I merely selectively gazed. The effect however was devastating. The man immediately ceased gazing and began to gawp like a mouse turned up under the plough. His eye darkened with an abrupt and unawaited onset of thought, likewise with some anger, the natural response of one who has just been ploughed up under the furrow. At this point I thought it best to depart. I brought the experiment to a halt, concluding that gazing is a purely one-way process, which presupposes non-reaction from the object of its gaze, and demands uninterrupted privacy. He that gazes will not bite. But one must not gaze back.

> ...Window-panes are sand once more
> Ink is water
> benches trees
> chalk again a cliff
> and a feather-pen is a bird
> JACQUES PRÉVERT
> 1947

Where You Do Absolutely Anything You Like

Between San Francisco and San José a special installation of the mass entertainment industry has been assembled and built, called Marine World Africa; it is a combined marine aquarium, zoological garden and amusement park. It costs just eight dollars, and there are no extras to pay, whether for touching a dolphin, or taking a ride in a boat, or seeing the chimpanzee, elephant and tiger show. This enables one to judge fairly definitively which are the best amusements on offer. In the amphitheatre set up for some sort of TV show about pirates (skulls, volcanoes, barrels of rum, one-eyed pirates and cannon at the ready) black-and-white killer whales obligingly leap up from the blue waters, in the pools one can view from above and below the blue whale, dolphins and divers, in shallow tanks one can stroke sea anemones and sea urchins, guarded against filching by a girl warden in a fetching uniform, nearby a few penguins huddle and seals and sea lions weepily bark, amongst the disporting public there pass more or less freely and easily llamas, buffalo, sheep and families of ducks, by boat one can visit the unbarred territory of lions and tigers, the second of which from lack of other things to do have just given birth to a world-record litter of eleven vigorous tiger cubs, in other aquariums one can photograph an unlimited multitude of tropical fish of select hues and patterns, and insofar as the surrounding nature fails to suffice, there is also on offer a superterrestrial monster of praeternatural size, something between an ox, an elephant, a serpent and a dinosaur, it does not move, but it is a film star right out of Star Wars.

Then for children there are swings, logs on a rope for crossing over the water, great enormous plastic punchbags to pummel and kick as much as arms and legs will stand, slides and dodgems, not to mention a trail through an extraordinarily jungle-like plastic jungle. And not to mention two tanks, holding up to waist height great piles of soft coloured plastic balls where you do absolutely anything you like, wade, dive, shriek, dig, flail, jump, fall, or stand on your head. Here it was we discovered that the most marvellous and amazing sight, over and above the dolphins and tigers and other tamed wonders, were five to a dozen children suddenly allowed to do absolutely anything they liked. Some couldn't quite believe it at first and had to be egged on by a girl with a microphone, but in the end they were all at it in a wild and somehow instinctive delight in motion limited by nothing but gravitation, in the collapse of all family taboos, in the liberated use of all their strength and all their might. These children are thus the only pure nature, unfeigned and unconfined and chock-full of joy. We said to ourselves, Man is a truly interesting species. It's just a pity that outside places like Marine World Africa these plastic tanks filled with balls aren't generally available.

We feel that even if all possible scientific questions be answered, the problems of life have still not been touched at all. Of course there is then no question left, and just this is the answer. The solution of the problem of life is seen in the vanishing of this problem.

LUDWIG WITTGENSTEIN
Tractatus Logico-Philosophicus, 1961

The intellect of man is forced to choose
Perfection of the life, or of the work.

W.B. YEATS
1933

Our Tiniest Nature Reserve, *or:* A Little Bit of Lyricism

On the edge of Prague, where a new town is rising through the muddy dusty wasteland, the bulldozers have shifted hummocks into hollows and hollows into hummocks, the mechanical diggers have carved out great ditches on the sites of future streets and the lorries have transported the slabs for thoroughfares which perish before our very eyes. On the few remaining islets of meadow remnants of hares crouch in confusion, peewits in spring cry over the denuded clover, scaring away the scrapers, and on the margin even the ploughman still toils for his grain. Pheasants conduct their young through the sewer pipes. If our nature writer Jaromír Tomeček could see it, he would pen a typically sad essay on the hopeless struggle of Wegwarte (chicory) with burdock, and shrews with the municipal grid.

Bearing in mind of course that a life of wait by-the-wayside is not a life of ease.

Nonetheless, in the willow bushes by the stream someone has fashioned a crystal spring for the passing wayfarer; water drops through a bark pipe into a stone receptacle, a little osier railing, a small plank shelf where mustard glasses for drinking are reinstated, for of old the weary pilgrim has taken these as souvenirs of his excursion. When the land about was still untouched by civilisation, every Monday the spring was lovingly restored after the weekend depredations, for this way led a path to a pond and a wood (mushrooms, campfire sausage, song of birds).

By some allowance of fate this one spot has remained unsullied, a microscopic islet amidst the pilings of earth. The willows, the spring of water, like a last living eye on a dead face. An eye with a railing and mustard glasses. What a triumph of tender care and beauty over pitiless steel and concrete! What a thumping of the heart when you listen with your ear to the ground!

Even if one cannot altogether ignore the fact that during the week the bulldozer men come and use the spring to cool their beer.

Nonetheless it is, so to speak, the tiniest nature reserve in the world. Even water-cress (Nasturtium officinale) grows here, providing green in winter and salad throughout the year.

I follow with trepidation the existence of this reservation week by week. It would take just one snatching grab of the digger. One caterpillar track. But there it still is, the water bubbles and the water-cress believes that next year will be the year of the water-cress. The willows believe that next year will be the year of the willows. The members of the housing cooperative wait for their flats. I wish for them that next year will be the year of the members of housing cooperatives.

But I think that the future street ought to be just as fine and just as human a place as this spring of water with its mustard glass service. And it ought to be called By the Spring of Living Water.

Go and compare yourself with man.
NIKOLAY VASILIEVICH GOGOL'
1809-52

A Conversation in the Woods

It was snowing. The woods recalled ancient woods and the dusk recalled ancient night. Next to an isolated cottage, between the hen-house and the rabbit hutch, an elderly man stood with a fur cap, a tender eye, and voluminous slippers. He was talking to his livestock, as right-minded people are wont to do. When we greeted him, he stepped up to us and engaged us in conversation.

Would we take a word of enlightenment. Yes, gladly. Did we know that good comes back to one. We did not. But it does, he said, it comes to the head of the bed in the evening. Aye, and it comes to the foot in the morning. It comes in the bread and in the water and in the word of the law.

And did we know, he said, that the way to the light is open. One must only repent of one's evil deeds and errors and guiles, one must only ask after the meaning of things, think earnestly and unstintingly, and then the thought keeps watch over us and the light enters in at the end of every journey.

Then he spoke of the man who hearkened to the voice of righteousness one day on the WC, for elsewhere he was ashamed to hear the voice of righteousness.

Then he spoke of his sons, who had strayed from the path, except for one, who still visited him, even though he was left all alone and the forest path was scarcely passable for two-track vehicles.

Then he showed us the way to the main road and watched us go, and his eyes faintly shone after us.

Then he vanished in the gloom.

We affirmed on the one hand that it was a pleasant form of schizophrenia. In any event every kind of schizophrenia is more pleasant in the woods than in the tram.

We affirmed however on the other that had we met in the woods Francisco Pizarro, just after he had grabbed the treasure of the Incas, torturing their king Atahualpa and slaughtering ten thousand serfs, we would most likely have seen him as just plain ordinary Francisco Pizarro. And if we had met a drunken Francisco de Benalcazar, just after he had had all the Indian dignitaries of Quito roasted over a slow fire, we would have seen him as a perfectly plain and ordinary Francisco de Benalcazar, merely a little obfuscated in his geography.

Only the man of tender eye, voluminous slippers and humble meditations on good and evil, the man who, on being met in the forest twilight longs to enlighten, appears to us as nutty as a fruit-cake.

We adjudged that, however correct the diagnosis, the error was in us, and there we were, thinking earnestly and unstintingly about the meaning of things, when the main road appeared between the trees. And it appeared to us, that it was a very ancient road, connecting Cuzco and Sachahuamen, while farther to the south-east the waters of great Lake Titicaca sounded, thawing the filtering snowflakes.

When I was a boy of 14 my father was so ignorant I could hardly stand to have the old man around. But when I got to be 21, I was astonished at how much he had learnt in 7 years.

MARK TWAIN
1835-1910

In Praise of Porters

The institution of porters is frequently the target of humorous remarks, even comic scenes. I too have never particularly warmed to porters, or rather to the procedures they demand of one before letting one into their building. I must admit however that I know of many institutions, of higher learning for example, where there used to be a porter and is no longer, and where the visitor misses this presence. Instead of the earnest, sometimes even kind solicitude of the man in the official cap the visitor is welcomed by the emptiness of the entrance lobby. Unregistered and unperceived he embarks on his tour of the building, unable to shake off the sense of being lost and out of place. The corridors become a labyrinth and there resounds in the distance the muffled roar of the Minotaur. The unobserved visitor may easily be engulfed by the dark historical recesses without ever being missed. The undirected visitor may easily go off down the garden path and never reach Senior Lecturer N.N.'s sought-after nesting place. Indeed, a visitor not taken in hand by a porter hardly exists at all in the first place.

How different it is in buildings still rejoicing in porters. The porter gazes with flashing eye out of his cubicle and at once bids the visitor to present himself and render up an account of his aims and intent. The visitor inscribes his name in a book and receives basic instruction in how to proceed on his way. Senior Lecturer N.N. is on the second floor, round the corner to the left of the stairs, Room 249. He has of course just gone to lunch. I remember porters who would expatiate on the finer details of a visit, supplying information even on the current mood of the said N.N., on the appropriateness of the visitor's wish to have himself orally examined on this particular day – I wouldn't if I were you, he's failed two already – likewise on the weather, the structural state of the building and the canteen food. Such porters give the building and institution a pleasantly cosy aspect, even a human face. I remember many a porter from edifices where I have long since forgotten the likes of Senior Lecturer N.N. The porter you see is unique, whereas there are any number of N.N.s, so that the porter is for all visitors the one central landmark, the common denominator of all one's errands and visits. The kind porter receives and places in safe keeping, sometimes even passes on, notes and sundry items, becoming an important link in the chain of human communication, bypassing the parlous state of the post office and telephones.

I must also allow that porters, unlike senior lecturers, are well-balanced, harmonious persons totally at one with their assigned station in life. This I ascribe to the circumstance that the human mind is better adapted to guarding a building and watching over an institution than for example to examining in crystallography. The human mind is better adapted to presiding over and above things in a cubicle than to getting mixed up in the nuts and bolts of the inner workings of buildings and institutions. Portering is a natural physiological state. And hence a worthy one. I have a nasty feeling porters are getting harder to find.

Edgar Degas purchased once
A fine El Greco, which he kept
Against the wall beside his bed
To hang his pants on while he slept.
RICHARD WILBUR
1950

How I Imagine My Readers

When New Year comes, one should basically reflect on matters. A scribbler for instance should basically reflect on how he imagines his readers, while the opposite must be envisaged also. I reflected and am only able to say I could imagine absolutely no one. Presumably I just simply write, and likewise just simply read.

Then I had to make a journey on the Prague metro, line C1. It happened that the tape-recorded message system on this particular train was somehow out of order. It had caught a chill or something and begun to slow down. After two stations it was croaking in an incredible deep bass. Keep clear of the sa-fe-teee---zo--one----the ---do---ors---are-----clo--------. The final syllable was so long in coming that at Pankrác Station a couple of limping old ladies still had time to get on the train. In the carriage itself the fantastic bass voice production had a most notable effect. It had the effect, as one would say in biology, of a differentiating or discriminating factor. The randomly dispersed passengers, contemplating the walls, atmosphere or nothing, were all sprung as it were into present life by this unexpected variety item, and stimulated into involuntary personal responses. Some began to exchange looks with one another, displaying happy amazement. Others simply began to laugh, although it is hard to laugh overtly, indeed aloud in an anonymous situation of mass solitude. Still others drew themselves up, frowned and glowered darkly. At Budějovická Station precisely the same passengers reacted in precisely the same way, except that the second, the overtly hilarious group, was already expectant, and one young man even decided not to get off, in order to enjoy the pleasant excitement. At Kačerov, the terminus, where all passengers were requested to alight, only the darkly frowning alighted immediately in disgust, whereas the others waited for the bass voice to finish its piece and made the whole train shake with delighted mirth. Which attracted considerable attention on the part of the supervisory staff, for a train shaking with delighted mirth is not a regular event round these parts. After the last syllables had expired all left the train with merriment on their faces and still looking back in gratitude.

And it was here, amongst these entirely unknown people, that I realised this was how I imagined the readers of these and other suchlike lines of writing! I imagine them just like those unknown faces which light up when instead of the usual official automated message a bass voice croaks at them in the tunnel. I imagine them like those who cause the train to shake with mirth, even though – or maybe because, the tape-recorder has gone on the blink. Like those who do not become solitary, although they are alone in a train. Their shell is permeable and porous. There are no words for the darkly frowning. For them I suppose there are only nutcrackers as for second-class walnuts.

The emotion of art is impersonal.
And the poet cannot reach this impersonality
without surrendering himself wholly to the work to be done.
T.S. ELIOT
1919

The Jingle Bell Principle

When receiving a visit it is proper to entertain it not only with solid and liquid refreshment but also with sound. For this reason every good household possesses a record-player or tape-recorder, whose canned music, frequently stereophonic, fills the space and relieves the members of the feast of the obligation to seek to converse. If conversation does take place it is uttered in a melodramatic manner to a background of popular or so-called serious music. Conversation on the supply of the market with spare parts for this and that to the accompanying strains of the Kreutzer Sonata is doubtless one of our supreme cultural blessings. Sooner or later, the reproductive music-synthesising system itself becomes the subject of conversation, and the visitors are thus regaled not only with cultural delights but also with technical enlightenment. I have repeatedly witnessed situations where the proud host has merely displayed his loudspeakers and tapes without making any actual application of them, thereby documenting the fact that for the up-to-the-minute man of the hour the essence is not so much in the music as it is in the apparatus. I have never yet encountered a situation where the host has displayed his new microwave oven but failed to serve any coffee. I dare say coffee is in some sense more basic to modern society than music.

It once happened all the same that a number of up-to-the-minute people from various scientific and technological fields, normal, adult and competent, came together in a chalet which had no equipment for reproducing music. One of these, a well-known electron-microscopist, had evidently anticipated or at least now felt the lack of acoustic entertainment and unpacked – not a portable tape-recorder,

nor a transistor radio, nor even a harmonica – but a plain ordinary jingle bell. A large shiny jingle bell the size of a quail's egg, with slots and openings, the kind you might find on Punch's cap or the skirt of the dancer Esmeralda. There was a great benevolent nocturnal silence, with only the sound of an ambulance siren or something coming from afar, not a bird cheeped nor any clamour of drunken Danes reached our ears: silence. The electron microscope man shook the jingle bell and a sweet, tenuous, delectable sound tinkled out, a delicate silvery laughter in the great pool of darkness. He shook the jingle bell upwards, sideways and downwards, altering its sounds and final tinkling cadence. Then he spoke of the ways of jingle bells and the techniques of sounding them, and all of the company tried out the bell in question. And that was it.

I can only say it was a great acoustic experience. Perhaps even a great musical experience. About experiences there is nothing more to be said, but there is just one thing I should like to add, that it is only to those still able to delight in a jingle bell tinkling in the dark of night that hi-fi equipment means any more than a microwave or a fridge.

...singing despite the gods and croaking toads
one cicada more
or one cicada less
HANS MAGNUS ENZENSBERGER
1957

On Inward Humming

Mental life consists, according to the textbooks, of thought and feeling, according to the poets, of addressing an inner voice (or voices), and according to the dramatists, of internal monologues. In my experience however it consists mainly of intermittent silences, and humming. Humming accompanies habitual and semi-automatic activities, as well as stoppages. Humming accompanies a sort of incomplete concentration on things around one, as well as a sort of incomplete concentration on oneself. Humming is characteristic of psychological states in which we are not exactly miserable, and states in which we are not exactly ecstatic. Which amounts I think to more or less always.

There are three grades of humming. The first is totally quiet and imperceptible. A tune simply runs in our head and leaves traces, in which another tune approaches, or the same one again, twice or ten times over. In the second the humming is still covert, but accompanied by a certain residual degree of motor activity: by a gentle tapping of anything against anything else, in other words, by a teeny little tippety-tappet. Accompanied by a delicate rhythmic pulse. Accompanied by motion of the lips, otherwise dumb. In the third type the humming is overt, mainly consisting of gentle whistlings under the breath and croonings, something the hummer finds as congenial as his immediate neighbourhood finds it irritating, being itself either in the middle of a pause or humming away to another tune, regarding one's own as a pernicious intrusion.

Humming to oneself is an activity as private as it is infectious and hard to resist. If you are infected first thing in the morning by the Duke's aria from Rigoletto it will still be busily at it at bedtime, at a time when your attitude to life is really very far removed from that of the said Duke of Mantua.

All this suggests to one the fundamental and underestimated importance of mental humming in the musical life of the nation, in the psychology of human congregations and in the mentality of the individual. The delver into the mind, or more specifically the psychiatrist, ought to interest himself just as much in covert humming as in dreams, the sociologist ought to concern himself with the ruling hummed ditties of a given era and area. And those who create music, serious or otherwise, might study with profit their public's inner musical repertoire.

In my opinion our local repertoire of inward humming still consists mainly of folk tunes, floating about freely and spontaneously in the mind. The melodies of operetta and the dance hall, and especially of brass bands crop up more often in stress situations and obsessively, in the manner of fixed nightmare images.

Fragments of symphonic compositions and the ubiquitous rock music, spirituals and their like occur more often as the consequence of a certain musical effort, as a kind of internal concert performance, accompanied by little dreams about how we would perform it on stage.

I wonder what Walkmans will do to this essential human condition. For my own part, I see them as obsessive stranglers of our own obsessive inner music.

In any event, I view those who hum to themselves as basically one of us. Those whom I have never detected humming to themselves I consider to be a strange species of unknown biology.